Iduma's prose is always fresh
ing, and evocative, *The Sound of Things to Come* marks him as a
unique talent to watch.

—Ayobami Adebayo, *Stay With Me*

The gradual revelation of the connections between the disparate
lives in Iduma's adventurous novel illuminates the unpredictable
workings of our common humanity and compels us to confront
our shared vulnerabilities. Privileging the road less traveled in its
aesthetic choices, *The Sound of Things to Come* is an essential read
for anyone interested in unconventional fictional investigations
of contemporary experience.

—Rotimi Babatunde,
winner of the Caine Prize for African Writing

Like an expert charmer, Iduma strings the reader along with
delectable character portraits, building anticipation until the last
page. *The Sound of Things to Come* announces the arrival of another
talented writer.

—Abubakar Adam Ibrahim,
The Whispering Trees and Caine Prize nominee

In *The Sound of Things to Come* Emmanuel Iduma deploys a
meta-psychological technique where his characters are dissected
for both experiences and motives. The innards of his characters
are exhibited as though for contemplation... And in spite of this
experimental foray, their humanity is left intact.

—Dami Ajayi, *Clinical Blues*

THE SOUND OF THINGS TO COME

Emmanuel Iduma

THE MANTLE

New York

A version of this novel was first published in Nigeria under
the title *Farad* by Parrésia Publishers in 2012.

This book is set in Gill Sans MT and Palatino Linotype.

Cover art by Victor Ehikhamenor of Nigeria (victorehi.com).
Cover design by Tijana Cvetkovic (tijanacvetkovic.weebly.com).
Interior design by Susan Leonard (roseislandbookworks.com)

978-0-9965770-9-0

Printed and bound in the United States of America by
McNaughton & Gunn, 960 Woodland Drive, Saline, MI 48176.

THE MANTLE

21-33 36th St.
Astoria, NY 11105
mantlebooks.com | @TheMantle

...precious warning: don't forget that all is not here... behold the innumerable, listen to the untranslatable.

—Hélène Cixous, *Là Venue l'écriture*

In the end, that was life: a few plates, a favorite comb, a pair of slippers, a child's string of beads.

—Jhumpa Lahiri, *Unaccustomed Earth*

However the image enters / its force remains within my eyes...

—Audre Lorde, *Afterimages*

THE SOUND OF THINGS TO COME

One

THE MEMORY BAND

I

He suddenly realized she had been watching him; he figured she must have been there for a while, seeing as she stood like a supervisor of his existence, with hands across her chest, eyes unblinking. Before he looked up to see her, his head had been bent, eyes fixed on the pile of examination papers he had been grading. On feeling he was being watched, he raised his head and saw she was there, right in *his* office. He wondered fleetingly how she had managed to get past the door without his notice; he wondered again how long she had been watching him. In seeing her, he held something past—a memory he would rather forget. Even when he stood, matching her height with his but avoiding her gaze, he was unable to comprehend how it was that he felt taken-hold-of, smeared with the irreversibility of previous years. And even when he said her name in a quiet mutter—as though it were taboo—he still felt haunted. "Goody."

"Your office looks good."

"Did you have a hard time finding me?"

"No, of course not. Your name is on the door."

In the curiously animated mental space in which he found himself, he realized next that they were both, somehow, sitting—she on the hard chair across the desk. He felt she was close enough even there—too close already.

"It's been a while," Goody said.

"Yes."

"You have not changed. Not a bit."

"Me?"

"Yes."

"Oh."

She looked at him and smiled. He took his time to look at her too. Not at her eyes yet: at the other parts. There was something familiar about that red blouse and those jeans. Were they not what she had worn on that day, three years ago? But they couldn't be. Would she come to his office in the same clothes she had worn on the day she left his house?

"I like your blouse," he said.

"Thanks. I was in a hurry. I didn't think it would impress."

"Do you want anything?"

"Anything?"

When she asked, he began to think that anything could mean a drink or her purpose for coming. Why had she come to him?

"I missed you. Really," she said.

"Really?"

"Really."

"I didn't imagine you would."

In saying this he did not look at her—he still dared not look into her eyes. Convinced he lacked guts, he did not dare match her constant gaze while making a statement he believed to be true. Surely he couldn't have imagined she would miss him after what she said the last time they were together. She hadn't called him a fool, she hadn't said anything unspeakable. She had said simply, "I'm leaving you." There was neither a kiss nor a hug to accompany her departure. He didn't deserve such a keepsake—something to hold onto. She was leaving, as she said, with nothing left *for* him. She was taking all of him, away.

"I came here because of my sister."

"Ella?"

"Yes."

"Is something wrong?"

"Yes. Yes, Frank."

He turned over an examination booklet that was open on his table, slowly, so the back cover with the university crest faced him. It had been open even before Goody came into his office; he looked at it with renewed interest, intent on drawing his eyes away from her—but it didn't last. He caught himself looking at her red blouse, and then up. He saw that her head was bent and felt the temptation to ask her to leave—he didn't want to share in her concerns, in *any* of her life.

"She's not talking to anyone," Goody said, as though the words weighed a stone each.

Frank asked, "Is that a problem?"

"Frank!" she called in exasperation.

"What?"

"She's not talking. She stays in the room almost motionless. She does not care for herself, about anything. Isn't that a problem?"

"Well, from my POV, it's not a problem."

"You're crazy, Frank. And what's POV?"

"Point of View."

"You are as crazy as your point of view then."

He did not see the point of having a fight with someone he once loved, who once left him, and who, coming back to his office three years later, called him crazy.

"Well, you can leave a crazy person's office."

"Frank. Please."

"What do you want from me?"

"Come and see her."

He looked at her tight-fitting top; it was the only thing he wanted to think about: her blouse.

II

Ella did not see the wind. Rather, it called to her, speaking the two syllables of her name precisely. Yet when she turned, she could not find it. Those who saw her look to the window did not see the wind either, and they did not know it called her. To them, Ella's out-worldliness became defined the moment she looked at the window.

The three of them stood watching. Ella sat on the bed with her back to the wall. Frank and Goody stood, silently watching, while her mother, Mrs. Anjola, clasped her hands to her chest as she sobbed. All Ella did was listen to the wind and try to see it. So when she spoke four sentences without pause, Goody and Mrs. Anjola were in disbelief. She said, "God has a prerogative to grant relief to an undeserving world. The apostles of merciless-ness and their cohorts came to me. My name was mispronounced and misspelled by a male hag." The three bystanders turned to each other, shaking their heads in unison. It was not out of pity. It was out of something more, for pity had determinable param-eters—you could tell what was pitiable. But they shook their heads for something without definition. Ella had become to them something beyond parameters—like a unicorn that could not be conjured. But then, while they were examining the parameters of the *thing* that exceeded pity, she spoke her last sentence, as if hastily tacked onto the previous ones, "Frank Dimkpa."

Frank turned. He felt as though he was being summoned to defend his name—was Frank even his name? To be called by her was to be summoned by other-worldly beings. She said nothing beyond that. Not another word. Her accomplishment suggested that no new words could do better than these. Frank, sensing he was of no use in the room, having been rendered witless when he

4

heard his name called by Ella, walked out. Goody followed, leaving her mother to resume her sobbing and watch an Ella whose eyes were fixed nowhere, or perhaps fixed on the spot where the wind might appear.

"Frank," Goody called when he was in the hall. There was a sense of mishap in his mind, the sense of how things could be pulled instead of turned. How could he explain the world turning around on a coin because his name had been called by a traumatized woman—his ex-student? Only then did he hear Goody call his name. "Frank. Help me."

"You haven't told me why I should. Why is it me you're coming to?"

She paused. The snarl beneath his question was formidable, like a truck on the highway stopping her from crossing the road when her life depended on doing so.

"I have no reason."

"So, let me leave." He was at the front door; his hand on the knob.

"She was your student, Frank."

"I know."

"She just called your name."

When he didn't say, "I know," as she had expected, she seized the opportunity. "This is not the first time you'd do something without reason. It might be fate."

"What's fate? You came to me in my office to help your sister. I'm not a therapist. I'm nothing. So what's fate here? Why should I help? You give me no reason. Why am I here?"

She said, in response, "That's the question you should be asking."

He turned the knob finally, let himself out, and banged the door behind him.

5

III

Frank mocked fate. When he told his landlady how he had been called to help a traumatized woman, and how he saw no sense in that call, he laughed. He laughed while he told her of what had happened, shaking his head to suppress the sense of guilt tugging at his heart. But Debbie, who knew him quite well, having lived with him for three years and having been friends with him for much longer, knew when he was lying. She knew this from the insincerity of his laughter. His lightless face told her he was being dishonest—that there was a deep longing in his heart created by the Anjolas that he needed to fill. His landlady knew the time had come for him to fill that longing, that he was a wanderer whose homecoming was imminent. So she said to him in her best motherly voice, the sort that compelled listening, "You can help her."

"What?"

"You heard me."

She saw him look at her husband's photograph hanging on the wall. He wore an academic gown—the photo had been taken at his inaugural lecture, two weeks before his death. She, defying his death, gave hers a month later on schedule, even though her friends had called her insane, emotionless, how-could-you-have-no-respect-for-his-memory? The title of her lecture was "The Underbelly of a Mental Patient," in which she had hoped, as she wrote, "to chart the moral career of a mental patient, and to question whether mental patients are not saner than pre-patients—those who assume they are well and need no attention." As expected, it blew the dust off the field, shamefaced those who had thought her insensitive. Her husband's death had been a trigger; it had given her the resolve to ask questions. Now, looking at Frank assertively, she saw how easy it was for him to cover his true feelings, how difficult it was for him to uncover them.

"Don't look at Leke's picture. Look at me." He turned.

"I don't care what you say. I can't help her. I mean, I don't know how to help her. She says rubbish, she's mad. I'm a philosophy teacher. I'm no psychiatrist."

She could have said to him, "We are all psychiatrists." Her major contribution to the field was that everyone could heal, with the right words spoken, the right action taken, with the right mindset. Frank was different. But she said instead, "You know her. She was your student. What's wrong with her is not beyond your reach."

"Why did she call my name?"

"She loves you. You've been in her head all along."

"That's not funny."

But he laughed at the ingenuity of her joke. He stood up after the calming laughter was spent. Debbie understood. He sometimes took such unexpected actions—biting his phone after a call, slapping himself on the head, pocketing his hands immediately after shaking hands with someone. She saw him look around the living room, and although that seemed to be another of his unexpected actions, they locked eyes and shared a silence-in-looking. It was a modest room. Two long settees, a 14-inch television, a record player (covered in dust) connected to two speakers. There was a table on which sat a bouquet of plastic flowers, the only recent thing in the room. The furniture and décor was outmoded, as though Debbie's reality was the past, as though she were more present in her past than in the present.

"How can I help her?" he asked.

"Bring her here. There's a spare room. We'll feed her, give her the right environment."

"We?"

Debbie laughed. "I want to be of use."

"This is crazy. I don't understand. There's something incomprehensible about this."

Debbie said nothing. She patted her hair; it was greying. She felt the same way about her life. It wasn't black, or white. But grey.

IV

As if on cue, Goody called as soon as he was in his room. "You have my number?"

"I kept it."

"Oh. That's strange. I mean, after leaving me."

"Don't mock me."

He felt he was talking to her in person, and her voice was her face and he could see every expression she made. Perhaps this was what had necessitated their apartness, the inevitability of attack—each would pounce on the other. Surely to love was to be *defensive*, not offensive. Yet, both of them hurled things at each other. They made weapons of words. They made lasting scars.

"So, what do you want?"

"You don't know what I want?"

"Okay. You'd have to thank Debbie. She talked me into doing it."

"Debbie?"

"Have some respect. She's a professor of psychiatry!"

"Ha ha."

She was "Debbie" to him, as simple as it sounded. If he called her Professor Debola, it would complicate things. Their relationship would be strained.

"With all the fight you have in you, you should be able to help your sister. You don't sound desperate. You sound unhelped."

"Unhelped? There's no word like that."

"Ha ha. I forget you're an English major."

"You know we don't call it 'major' in Nigeria because there's nothing like a minor degree in our educational system. You forget.

Who's the fool now?" She was still her old self, he thought. She remained composed in discomfiture. Who would imagine her sister was out of her senses, and that the present telephone call had been made to seek healing?

"Ha ha. That's all I can say. You're the fool, and you know."

"Shut your big mouth! What's your plan for Ella?"

"Debbie thinks we can keep her here. In our place. So we'll come and get her."

There was a pause on the line. He heard her begin to sob.

"Don't be a child. Thank me."

"For what?" she said, with an unclear voice.

He said ha ha again, she called him a fool, and he realized she was the only person he could say ha ha to without feeling childish or nitwitted. Then he ended the conversation, and felt foolish.

V

Yes. Ella finally saw the wind. She felt exuberant, like a child who had found a long-lost toy. When Goody and Frank entered her room—which had white curtains and walls bearing the marks of stripped-off wallpaper—she said to them, "I can see the wind." Both had no ready words. Goody looked at Frank and Frank looked at Goody, thinking the same thing. In her presence, though, they knew they had to act sane.

"Ella," Goody said, "We're taking you out."

"Is this a movie?" Ella asked, smiling.

"What?" Goody asked.

"You say you're taking me out. I'm asking you if this is a movie. Simple." And she smiled again, then hissed, then smiled yet again. Frank was irritated. There was a thrust of reality in the moment. He considered himself a fool to have thought that it was merely a matter of telling her to move and she would move.

"What do you want, Ella?" Goody asked, in a matter-of-fact, exasperated tone. It didn't work. Ella did not respond. Then Goody turned and looked at Frank, whose hands were pocketed. His eyes were fixed on a curtain. Perhaps he also saw the wind.

"Frank," she whispered.

"What?" Frank asked, carried away by his thoughts.

"Frank!" she screamed. And Ella turned to them. Frank, seeing his disenchantment angered Goody, moved toward Ella. He was not thinking, he was acting by instinct and by whatever else, so that his action, when considered later, would have the quality of right and wrong in equal measure, of a mistake and a miracle. He took Ella by the left hand and began to pull her away from the bed. Goody stared, too awestruck to speak. Surprisingly Ella made no sound. When he saw that she gave no opposition, he said, "Easy. We're taking you out of here," and released his tight grip, holding her more gently. When they got to the living room, where Mrs. Anjola was sitting, her fingers interlocked over her head, Ella began to talk loudly, hurriedly, appealingly.

"Don't take me to him. You can kill me. Do anything! Don't take me to him!"

The mother, deficient in handling emotions, began to wail, "Don't take her anywhere!" Goody, knowing her mother, implored Frank onward. "Go ahead." By this time, Ella's movement was snail-like, and Frank had to pull her. He thought of nothing, only of Ella's movement, of how he could get her into his car. And he did. When he, Ella, and Goody were in the front seat of the red Subaru, Ella suddenly went quiet. Frank turned to see if she was alive. Had she suddenly dropped dead? She hadn't, of course. She was just sitting still, between Frank and Goody, her hands between her legs. Her face was fixed, but her eyes glistened, as though she was going to cry. Goody, sitting beside her, began to sob.

"Don't be a baby," Frank said, but his tone was inappropriate—he said it only to relieve his tension. As a matter of fact, he wanted to *relive* the tension, for suddenly, with Ella's silence, he felt useless. Conflict had abated. He was prepared for far too much a confrontation to be content with just a little. Goody quieted. There was no fight in her this time. Frank drove the car in silence. There was only the noise of Goody's occasional sobs. He wished there was more noise, more of a fight, more *Ella*.

VI

In July, Ife had the character of an excited toddler. The toddler was everywhere, and in everyone. A residue of that excitement was evident in every talk, every walk. Yet Frank sensed dizziness, one that followed a large meal, and asked Debbie in her office, "Is it good that the Head of State died?" Debbie, being who she was, was unaccustomed to yes or no. In her reckoning there was no yes or no, as there was no white and no black, only several in-betweens.

"I can't say."

She was not thinking what he was thinking and this annoyed Frank. He sensed that she was operating on a different frequency from him, that he could not confide in her or tell her his thoughts.

"You're not listening to me."

"Of course," she said, and pushed back her oversized glasses.

She was packing her books into a sack on which was printed "Infinite Grace: God sells, we buy." The slogan had always amused Frank, but now it did not.

"That's a stupid tagline," he said. Debbie did not reply. "Where do they buy from God? Does God sell anything?" He stood up, still talking.

"You know what?" Debbie retorted. "You're a big baby. What's annoying you?"

"You," he said flatly, and walked away.

He started toward his department. His car was in the parking lot outside the philosophy building, a twenty-five-minute walk. With every second that passed, he felt increasingly witless—as though there were a billion droplets of insanity in his head. All he could think of at first was "God sells, we buy." It rang in his head like the noise of rushing water, until it became "God buys, we sell."

So he walked on under the scorching sun—an enemy. There were enemies everywhere—the students holding books or carrying papers in their back pockets; the morose lecturers trudging to classrooms. He couldn't fathom what made things into an enemy for him; it would be easy to think it was his anger at Debbie's inability to reach out to him, to answer his questions in the manner he wanted them answered. But he knew it was something deeper. The real source of his angst was Ella, who had been brought into their lives just yesterday. Debbie brought supper for Ella last night and then ordered the maid to ensure there was always food for her. Frank left the house this morning without saying anything to Ella, without doing anything for her.

When he got to the parking lot he chose to keep walking, deciding that he'd pick up his car the next day. Behind the Department of Philosophy was a path that led to the Faculty of Agriculture, which in turn led to the university's staff quarters. He lived with Debbie in one of the closer houses, so he could walk.

A car pulled up beside him: Debbie. His anger was rekindled.

"I'll meet you at the house," he said. She didn't implore him. She moved on, and the car soon receded from his view. He wished, suddenly, that Debbie could recede from his life. But he knew that would remain only a wish.

When he was a couple of streets away from home, a 340 GL Volvo pulled up beside him. Goody was driving. By now he was drenched in sweat. It was illogical to refuse her ride; he knew she was heading to see Ella. As he got in the car she turned off the engine. She seemed to be waiting for something to happen. They stayed parked at an intersection. This is dangerous, Frank thought, but he felt comfortable, regardless.

"How's your husband? I haven't asked you."

"Oh."

"He's oh?"

"How's Ella?"

"You're mad." They laughed together.

"I don't know."

"Please, Frank."

"I'm not a psychiatrist. And it's only been one day!"

She looked sideways, out of the car window. But he had seen her tear-filled eyes.

"Goody." She did not turn to him. "Is there something I should know? About Ella?"

He saw that she could not bring herself to say yes. She raised her left palm to the steering wheel and, still avoiding his eyes, stared straight through the windshield. The problem, as Frank guessed, was that she saw herself too much in Ella's plight. It seemed that telling him what he ought to know was telling herself what she wanted to forget. In essence, Ella's story was her story. Even more, there was a part of Ella's story in which she considered herself guilty. And that part—that guilt-invoking part—curtailed her ability to tell him the story.

"Talk to me, Goody. I want to know what happened to Ella." Goody finally sighed and looked at Frank, breaking away from her escapist pose—she knew he would leave if he did not know. So she began to tell him the part of herself that was Ella.

VII

Ella appeared in her house on a public holiday, taking Goody by surprise. Goody was sitting on the veranda of her husband's house in the barracks. The time was possibly 4:00 pm. She was alone. Her husband, Chris, a brigadier, was not in, not that she expected him to be back that early.

"Emmanuella!" Goody called out to her, standing, even though Ella had dropped her small duffel bag and sat on the other chair on the porch. She felt that she was always unable to match her sister's stubbornness, her characteristic insistence. Sometimes Goody thought that the adhesive of their relationship was also the reason for their tension—that she was always unable to confront her sister properly, to fight a war that needed to be fought. So, that early evening, when Ella arrived unannounced, she called her name in full. In the depth of her subconscious, she figured that it was only by calling her "Emmanuella" that she could confront her dangerously insistent life.

"Goody," her sister called in return "Good afternoon."

"I didn't know you were coming."

Ella smiled, somewhat evasively. "No. I didn't tell you."

Goody laughed, "Let's go in." That was the only thing Goody could say. When they were in, Goody noticed that Ella was looking around the living room as though it was her first time there. She did not sit immediately, and Goody stood beside her. Now, she held her duffel bag with both hands and faced a large photograph of Chris. Ella smiled as she looked at this.

"Chris will be surprised to see you."

"Ah, yes. He will be."

After a brief silence descended on the living room, during which both sisters sat beside each other, Ella reclined back and said matter-of-factly, "I left school."

It was at that moment she realized that being six years older did not necessarily make her Ella's senior. She found many reasons to believe that being born before Ella was God's unrepentant mistake — an error He'd eternally regret. And so, when Ella said she had left school, Goody sighed and looked at her own photograph, beside her husband's, thinking while she looked that she should say something chiding, that looking at her photograph was vain, superficial, inconsequential.

"Well," Goody said, "why did you leave?"

"I was tired."

Goody turned to Ella to ask another question but the thought leaped from her head. The only question she could muster was, "Are you hungry?"

"Yes."

Ella stood up and headed for the kitchen. Goody followed her, as though she were the visitor.

Her husband returned too late to meet her resistance. Indeed, his returns had long been marked with a silence that had become her character. She was not the type of wife to accuse her husband of promiscuity. It was not that she was convinced of his fidelity; she believed it was her offhand reaction to his late homecomings that saved their marriage. But theirs, she surmised, was not a marriage. When she met him, a day before her convocation, she did not think of him as a potential husband. She thought of him as Frank's opponent, a man with whom she could be friends only to prove how incomparable he was to her partner. She was to spend the next month in Ife with her mother, planning her next move in life. It was a dangerous period, she'd realize later, for in transition one is too susceptible to change and this vulnerability is hard, often impossible, to detect.

On the day she met Chris, Goody was walking past the Department of Geology's parking lot and he was parking his car, a green Army-issued Peugeot. He called to her. She was surprised at his boldness and that her face, plain as it was, had mattered to him. She was on her way to the Old Bukateria, the university's food market, where she was hoping to find the vegetables her mother asked her to buy. When he said, "Hello ma," she immediately thought of how Frank would not call out to a stranger, of how his courtesy informed his social relations. She turned because of his uniform, as she wasn't sure if he could take no for an answer. A soldier at that time needed any excuse to denigrate a civilian.

"Yes?" she said, detesting that she considered his face a great sea of blackness.

"My name is Chris. Chris Lawanson."

"Okay, Chris. Can I go?"

"Oh yes. Of course."

"Thank you." But with the way he smiled, without a hint of defeat, she hesitated, struggling with her desire to walk away.

Seeing that his unabashed response to her curtness was working, he said, "I know you're in a hurry. I'd like to talk with you sometime. Say, tomorrow?"

"Okay," Goody said, and started to walk. His smile had begun to lose its charm.

He walked after her. "I'd like to take you out, tomorrow. Lunch."

She said to him, behind her, "Okay."

He said, "You keep saying okay. I need you to tell me yes. And where I'd meet you tomorrow. Please."

She stopped when he said "Please." It did not sound like if he was begging her. It sounded as though he was fetching from an already dug well, as though he was asking for what belonged to him, rightfully, legally.

"Meet me here at two."

"Tomorrow?"

"Yes."

She had agreed without thinking. She would often think of the affair as an error that had yet to be proved.

At the beginning it was his directness that surprised her, and she agreed to meet him only because she wanted to prove him wrong, to prove that she wouldn't leave Frank. Then some things led to other things, and she took him to her mother, who detested Frank's iconoclasm, and who warned that iconoclasts were doomed to poverty and social irrelevance. She chose him for her fear of Frank's failure. She didn't think she possessed the ability to cope with his possible derailment, as much as she thought then that she loved him.

On the day that Ella arrived unannounced, her husband returned at midnight. They shared and unshared a room. He left to a smaller room whenever he detested her "kinship," as he called it. That night, when she sat on their king-size bed, she wasn't waiting. She was only awake, thinking too much about Ella's real reason for visiting—she could easily decipher a hidden agenda. Yet she knew she was speculating without proof.

The first thing she said to her husband was, "Ella is here."

"Oh. She came." It was a statement, not a question.

"Yes."

He undid his belt and hung it over his neck, as though he planned to use it later.

"That's the first thing you say to me?"

"Eh?"

"You heard me. You say 'eh' when you're guilty."

She snapped, "So I'm guilty?" immediately regretting it. He looked at her condescendingly, a look she knew preceded his anger and intolerance.

"Shut up," he said. By now he was wearing only his boxer shorts. She did not mind his saying "Shut up." What bothered her was what she perceived as his role in bringing Ella to their house, even in making her leave school. Of Ella's presence, he had said, "Oh. She came," as if he expected her.

"Why's Ella here?"

It was a direct question, and he answered directly, "I told her to come."

She had two reasons to justify her subsequent action. One, she felt embarrassed that there was an ongoing relationship between Ella and her husband, underground as it appeared, perhaps calculated to keep her in the dark. Two, she felt insulted, even assaulted, at his pride, his self-assertion, which she often considered profane. Who was he to ask her sister to come to Abuja from Ife, not caring if she dropped-out of school in the process? And for what reason? But at that instant, his reason did not disturb her; his avaricious pride did. She stood from their bed and stood up directly to him, faced him as though in a duel. Then she punched him in the stomach. His paunch was thick, leathery, and her fist bounced back. He reacted in mocking bemusement. This was the first time she had squared up to him physically.

His belt still hung over his neck. He slowly drew it from his neck while she stood looking at him, seeming to call his bluff. There was some drama—some grand Shakespearean allusiveness—in the way he drew the belt, looking at her with a vestige of that mocking bemusement. He raised the strap and she balked, although the flinch was in her eyes alone. The rest of her body seemed prepared for a whipping. At the last second, when her body had tensed in readiness for a lash from an Army belt and buckle, he restrained himself and smiled broadly.

"You're funny, Goodness."

He always called her Goodness; he'd told her once that he detested calling her Goody; it made her *sound* too good, too self-righteous, which she was not. She agreed with him on that point. He sat on the bed then threw the belt on the floor. She lived constantly on the fringe of violence. He had never hit her, but it could happen any day.

She felt stupid, exposed, more embarrassed by her attack than by his secret friendship with Ella. He laid back on the bed; his feet remained on the floor. She lay in the same fashion, and recognized it as one of the moments in which they came close to love, close to receiving a divine intervention in their romance. She said, feeling tender, wanting to be held, comforted, "I'm sorry."

"You don't have to be. I mean, you *should* be."

"Ha ha."

"You and your ha has."

"Ha ha," she said again, and he flung an arm at her belly. She winced, gratefully. It was an unexpected moment too, his childishness, a rarity from him. He always maintained a distance, a don't-speak-until-spoken-to relationship. But suddenly, on the night of Ella's arrival, he regained his playfulness, the part of him that displayed the triumph of a teenager who had been given an undue advantage. This seemed fishy to Goody, so she brought up the subject of Ella again, recognizing that Ella was her leech; her sister was in her memory.

Her voice was as courteous as she could afford. "Why did you ask her to come?"

Contrary to her fears, he answered almost apologetically. "Well, I wanted her to be of use."

"How?" she asked, trying modestly against her rising temper, to retain her courtesy.

"Well, I should have told you about our conversations. She has called me almost every day since the beginning of last month. She built up our friendship." He seemed too apologetic, and she hated it. And she hated it further that he was placing Ella in a bad light.

"What was she saying when she called you? She called your office?"

"My office, yes. She said she was tired."

"Tired?"

"Yes, tired. Your sister is more enchanting than you are."

"What do you mean?"

"Endearing. Convincing..."

It sounded as though he had said "promiscuous." She replied tartly, "That's a crazy thing to say."

"Ha ha."

"Shut up."

He mocked her, flung his hand on her belly again. "Now you see what it means to be at the receiving end of ha ha," he chided further.

But Goody was serious; his newfound childlikeness would not distract her. "How do you want her to be of use?" She said this knowing what job he did for his boss, although he had not told her outright. She just knew.

"Well. Well." He was not stuttering. He was almost silent, even though he had said "well" twice.

"What's well?" Both of them sat up like rising golems.

"Well, she's beautiful. You know. She's young. She's tired of school. She's adventurous." Goody's heart skipped, skidded, slued. Her sister was the subject matter. She could not believe this. Chris' statement was far-off, out of reach, intangible.

"Did she tell you she wanted to sleep around?" Again, being direct did not evoke any sudden reaction from him. It seemed that, unlike her, he had rehearsed their conversation. He was too ready, too experienced in defending himself. He was a soldier.

"Well, indirectly. Yes." He chuckled, "The way you use words!"

"God, I can't believe you're doing this. My sister!" Goody stood.

Chris remained in his sitting position. The clock chimed. It was 1:00 a.m.

"I want to sleep, Goodness."

"Jesus Christ. Chris!"

"I explained everything to her. It's not sleeping around as you call it. It's pleasure. Girls are pleasurable. Abacha wants them once in a while to him keep company. They distract him. Who knows what would happen if Abacha did not have the girls. He'd go crazy. We'd all suffer. You know." She didn't want to *know*, so she walked out of the room, preferring to sleep alone; her husband, if theirs was a marriage, had betrayed her.

VIII

Very early the following morning, Ella became a victim of Goody's morality. She was still sleepy, having first the blurriness of vision that being woken up brings, and then, when Goody introduced the subject matter admonishing her not to "let Chris deceive her," she became wide awake, conscious, even defensive.

"What?" she said, still lying on the bed in the large guest room. Goody sat beside her and while she talked, she lightly held Ella's right knee.

"I said you should be careful of Chris."

"Why?"

"You know why, Ella."

"Well, I don't know."

Goody heard Ella's "well" and felt betrayed by Chris, again. If he had the conversations with Ella he claimed to have had, it was no surprise she sounded like him.

"Why did you come?"

"You want to send me away?"

"Yes, if I have to, if it would save you from harm."

Ella chuckled. Goody felt disrespected, but recalled that God seemed to have mistakenly denied Ella the right to be older.

"To save me from harm?"

21

"Harm, yes."

"That's really funny. Can you save me from harm?"

Goody was using the wrong words. It wasn't the first time Ella caught her doing so. "You know what I mean, Ella."

"I can't know what you mean. I came here because, well, Chris promised me a job."

"A job!"

"Yes. I'm out of school. I have to work for a living, you know."

"Did he tell you what kind of job?"

"Yes and no."

Goody still held her sister's right knee; with her increasing exasperation, she tightened her grasp. Surprisingly, Ella did not protest.

"You traveled from Ife to Abuja for a yes-and-no job?"

"You're misunderstanding me." She said this with some laughter in her voice; Goody thought her tone to be scornful and it angered her even further. It was particularly annoying that she was looking out for Ella, who seemed to be looking elsewhere.

"Well, let me *understand* you!"

"Yes, he told me the general nature of the job. No, he didn't tell me what I'd be doing specifically." Again, Ella had a mocking tone in her voice, overtly suggesting that for her the conversation was a game of words.

"I'm serious about this, Ella."

"Well, I'm serious about this too."

"Can you stop using that word?"

"What word?"

"Well."

"Okay. Okay."

Goody bowed her head and rubbed her forehead. It was calculated to lessen the severity of the moment, to calm her nerves, maybe to catch herself from over spilling.

"What's the general nature of the job?"

"Well," she started to say—then she chuckled, caught her sister's eye, and became serious.

"He told me he could get me a job in Aso Villa. I'd be one of the domestic assistants to the Head of State. That's what he told me."

"Jesus Christ!"

"What?"

"It's amazing how Chris simplifies things. Domestic assistant! My dear, Chris is one of the closest aides to the Head of State. One of his official duties is to get mistresses for Abacha. You know, girls he'd sleep with. And I think this is what he wants to do with you."

Goody looked at her sister to see that she was shocked at the revelation of Chris's intent, to see her come to her senses and realize the wrongness of her ambition. But there was nothing in her sister's eyes. If anything, it was listlessness, a so-what? It took her almost a minute to express this apathy.

"Well, I can't be so sure."

"I'm sure, Ella, and I'm telling you."

"How are you sure?"

"I'm his wife for Christ's sake!" Exclaiming that way she was now over spilling, doing what she had hoped to prevent; she felt she would pour herself away in no time.

"It doesn't matter. Have you gone with him to pick the girls?"

"It doesn't matter whether or not I have gone with him to pick the girls."

"It does. You're being unbelievably categorical. Seeing is believing."

"That's biblically incorrect."

Ella laughed. "Yes. I see. You are very moral now. Very righteous."

"Ella, you shouldn't go with Chris."

"You know, I'm wondering how you've suddenly become moral. You that married Chris for his money. You that left Frank the way you did. Now you have the faint idea that I'll be sleeping with Abacha. I guess sleeping with Abacha is a greater wrong than getting married to Chris because of his money."

This outwitted Goody. She could only say, "I beg you, Ella. Don't go with Chris."

"Well, you have nothing to say to what I said? You agree, then. I'm asking you: which is a greater moral wrong—to sleep with Abacha or to marry a man because of his money?"

"This is crazy stuff you are saying, Emmanuella." Calling her name in full seemed the last logical thing for Goody to do, as though it was the means to a miracle—especially at a time when she felt outwitted. And, of course, as she knew Ella expected, she could not and would not answer. She knew a right answer might stop Ella from going out with Chris to Aso Villa. But was there a right answer?

"Well, it's crazy stuff you're saying too. I left school. I called Chris. I told him I was tired of Ife. He said I could come to Abuja. He'd get me something to do. Here I am. And you say I am here to sleep with Abacha. Even though I see the fallacy in your argument, I honestly do not care. I'm here. I'm here to do what I have to do."

Goody looked at her younger sister; she felt her sight was failing. She felt she was looking at Ella's shadow, or Ella's mirage, or some intangible Ella. So she only said, "Okay."

Ella sat up and held her sister's left arm, saying nothing. It was that moment Goody would remember and feel the guiltiest about—a moment when she failed as an older sister, the one who should know better. She recognized that moment as a confirmation of Ella's victory over her; for the way Ella had touched her seemed an assertion of superiority. Consequently, she felt limp

24

and dumb. When she got tired of feeling so, Goody stood, as Ella said, "I want to sleep more." She heard the clock in the living room chime seven. Then she heard the creak of Chris's door. She didn't think betrayal again; she thought loss, insignificance, worthlessness.

There was, as Goody liked to remember it, a glint of regret in Ella's eyes when she walked out of the living room to Chris's car later that morning, as though she had come to terms with her impending "job" in the Aso Villa. But Ella did not hesitate much. She held her small duffel bag in her right hand and a handbag in her left. Then she looked at Goody, who was sitting with her back straight. There was nothing in her voice that conveyed she was reconsidering. She said a simple "bye" to her sister, not smiling, although Goody flashed her teeth at her in a bid to simulate laughter.

Goody, while recalling that moment, would think of the sound of the car starting to move away, carrying Chris and Ella to Aso Villa. She sat there until she became tired from wishing things took a different turn. Then she went to the room she shared with Chris. Not thinking of his betrayal, she unexpectedly thought of their plan to have children, only two, starting from the fifth year of their marriage, which was two years away. She had entertained the thought, when they reached that consensus, that five years was too abstract. But now, as she lay down to sleep, she agreed to the idea. There was so much that could happen before then. For one, she could wake one morning and feel it was time to leave Chris. And there were the growing sensations that made her believe strongly in this possibility. She would look at Chris and find that he looked barely admirable to her; unlike the time she had decided it was him and not Frank, and had found some excuses for this decision. Other times she looked at him and detested his clean-shaven head and chin, and wishing that he kept an afro or left it punkish. Or even that he kept a goatee, a Herbert Macaulay-styled mustache, or that of Hitler's, or a Soyinka beard.

What would their child look like? Or children? Say, a boy, and then a girl? Or a girl, and then a boy? Would they have her oblong face, her brown eyes? Or would they have their father's looks? What kind of children would she and Chris make? What personalities would emerge from them? Would they have children with Chris's craftiness, his discipline? The thought of having a child for Chris, *with* him, appalled her that day and she fell asleep with the consolation that she hadn't become pregnant, would not become so in the coming year. She had enough time to sort herself out, find reasons to stay or leave, or stay and leave. The truth was she began to believe that her marriage was as much leaving as staying, that she was as much unmarried as married. She found no other thought appropriate, given what Chris was doing to Ella, and to her.

IX

Goody did not recount the recent past as if it came from her memory. She had been objective, telling her sister's story as though she was a stranger to it. Frank noticed this, but also noticed that when she got to the evening of Ella's departure she started fiddling with the steering wheel and her face twitched. Suddenly, she began to shed tears. Frank thought she was being a baby; he didn't see the point. And, as always, he felt he lacked the guts to do anything—say sorry, hold her, tell her it was alright. So he simply sat in her car and watched her cry.

She did not cry to her fill. She expected his voice to comfort her or to feel his arms around her. But since neither of these happened, she stopped crying altogether, as suddenly as she had begun. To half-cry was, in her opinion, inadequate; her release became unfinished. She became angry. And, of course, Frank was the only person she could take it out on.

"Leave my car, Frank."

Finding no reason to start an argument or a pleading-session, Frank slowly opened the door of the Volvo, as though he was waiting for her to call him back. But she didn't. She started the engine, reversed in quick, practiced moves, and the car sped away. Debbie's house was, at most, a minute's walk away. He turned and watched the car speed out of sight.

X

Frank did not like an open door. Yet, when he returned from talking with Goody, he was surprised to find the front door ajar. He knew Debbie had come in more than an hour earlier. He pushed the door and let himself in. From the living room he could hear Debbie's snore. He closed the door and sat down, weighing indiscernible options. He stood abruptly and in that instant the room appeared small in his eyes. He heard whistling and remembered that Ella was one of the reasons he was troubled. In the one day since she had been there, Frank had avoided her, staying out of the room in which she was kept. Consequently, he'd not spoken to her—but healing was impossible without speech. Although he knew this, and although he had rehearsed what he would say first—thinking of options such as "What's wrong?" "How are you today?" and "Talk to me"—the words were clumsy in his mouth. So he avoided her altogether.

Distracted by her whistling, he walked to the dining area, opened the refrigerator and pulled out a bottle of water. The liquid was cold and tasted bitter. He felt like a coward for taking the time to prepare himself to go to Ella's room. So, he put the bottle on the dining table and walked into the hallway that branched into Ella's room. All the rooms were on the left side of the hallway, four rooms in all. Ella was kept in the last and largest, room. It had been unoccupied since Debbie's husband passed away. Yet Debbie took the pain to clean it weekly, leaving his boxes of clothes, a black mourning cloth with a poorly drawn swastika on it, and his large black and white photograph hanging on the wall. Every time he had reason to enter the room, Frank felt the presence of someone, or *something*, as though the room was an annex of the afterlife.

When he entered that afternoon, it was more than an afterlife that stared him in the face. It was *the* afterlife. The swastika on the black fabric, drawn with a marker, had the quality of permanence. When Frank looked at it, hanging beside the black and white blowup of Debbie's husband, the swastika suddenly seemed able to regenerate itself. He saw thousands of swastikas made into one, such that when one disappeared another replaced it, like living cells. But taking his eyes away, he noticed the curtains. They bedeviled him, squashed him between life and eternity, whiteness and blackness. Then the bed on which Ella (*the* afterlife) sat staring at him was covered with a brilliant white bed sheet—white as though prepared for a lying-in-state.

It was Debbie's fault, Frank thought, standing as though waiting for something. Ella, no longer whistling, stared at him, as if she had drawn a sword for battle. Thinking that she was on the offensive, he had to be on the defensive. That was a mistake. So he sat beside her on the bed. Her hands were on her lap so that when she sat straight up, her back was like a slate. Her hands, folded on her lap, held nothing. Her fingers were interlocked. Even now, as he sat beside her, she turned her eyes and stared at him. Her brown eyes gave no inkling of her feelings—her eyes had the quality of being nothing and everything at once—he stared back and hoped to find a clue. Her glare was an act—or an art?—of battle.

He said, "Ella." Then he touched her hands on her lap, unlocked her fingers. It took some time before she reacted, counteracted even. In every skirmish, a pre-emptive strike is greeted with retaliation. Having understood her stare as a call to arms, Frank pushed himself into a battle he wasn't ready to fight. So when Ella began to scream, incoherently at first, he held her with increasing firmness. But then, out of her lips emerged coherence, "Don't touch me!" She screamed these words on and on, and Frank held his hands limply, as though waiting for action, for something to do with them. She wasn't screaming with an attitude; only her mouth moved. Her hands had returned to her lap, her fingers had become interlocked again. The shriek only came from her mouth, her body remained intact, unaffected by Frank's misadventure.

"Ella, please." The plea did not make a sound, given the volume of her scream. Debbie appeared. Her glasses were askew on her face. It was clear she had been disturbed from sleep. Ella screamed on: "Don't touch me! Don't touch me!" As soon as Frank saw Debbie, he stood, looking at her. Debbie looked back at him, and not at Ella. She kept her eyes on him, as though she was searching for the reason for Ella's screams on his face.

"Leave her," was all Debbie said. She flashed a glance at Ella, and then turned to look at Frank again. Frank still held his hands limply, as a soldier deprived of his armor and honor. His body was unwilling to yield to Debbie's command. Noticing this, Debbie went to him and pulled him by his hand. Ella was still screaming. He yielded to her pull, and as soon as the door was shut, Ella stopped screaming.

Frank, furious and defeated, walked to the living room, saying nothing to Debbie. He released himself from her grip as though she was Ella. He sat on one of the settees then stood immediately and went to the dining area where he found the bottle he had drunk from earlier still on the table. Some water remained in it. Still furious, he poured the liquid directly onto the table. He turned the bottle upside down and the last droplets joined the rest. He watched the water spill to the floor. They had no chance. He was failing with Ella.

Debbie came to him just as the dribbling water hit the floor. There wasn't a look of accusation in her eyes. If there was anything, it might have been a look of pity—of condescension even. She wore flannel pajama pants and an oversized t-shirt, on which was printed "University of California"—it had belonged to her husband. As soon as she stood beside him, he sat in one of the dining chairs. He looked at her and took his eyes away immediately. Her face was furrowed; he hated how she looked when she frowned. She sat down on the chair next to his and touched his hands, outstretched on the table in the paddle of water.

"You're not giving yourself to this, Frank," she said. He wanted to say something to nullify her point, to raise his voice and unbridle his emotions, but he felt constrained.

"She needs you. You're the only person from her past that can talk to her. She needs someone who can bring her to terms with the present."

"Is that why I'm doing this?"

"Yes," Debbie said, tightening her grip on his left hand.

"Well, it's crazy, because I don't know what to do. I want to do this. I have the feeling that I owe her something. She was a good student. And God knows I thought of her when she left… disappeared. I asked her friends if they had heard from her. No one said they had. Then Goody came and told me she needed my help. I want to help, Debbie. I just don't know how."

"Yes. I know Frank…"

"You understand me?" Something lifted from his chest. He felt a burden had been taken away, and he trusted Debbie to carry it.

"I understand you. You're trying too much. There is no fixed way. I studied psychiatry. What we do is find pattern in a pattern-less life. We meet someone today, we try to find a way to heal the person's mind. We meet again tomorrow. We *try* the same thing we did yesterday. If it works, it works. But we cannot predict the human mind."

"So, what do you want me to do?"

"Why are you doing this? You ask yourself first."

"I want her to be normal. Become the Ella I knew in class." Debbie bowed her head, smiling, and then she laughed.

"You want her to be normal? Is she abnormal?"

"Well, yes."

Debbie looked at him and grinned. This time she did not look at him with pity, but as one would look at a friend who knew too much, who was too intelligent. "Are you normal, Frank?" He did not answer, but he cracked a smile. She continued, "This is not about normalcy. This is about memory."

"What?"

"Memory."

"Oh. Memory."

"Yes. You should try to help her remember."

"Oh. Right."

"When she remembers, she'll *become* normal."

Frank fiddled with the bottle. He nodded. He looked at Debbie, at the wisps of hair that had become grey, and wondered what he'd do without her.

"Is that all?" he asked.

"All?"

"All I have to do?"

"Well, perhaps. It would be professionally incorrect for me to say yes. It's like we're trying to throw a net over flowing water."

"Oh, right." They heard Ella scream, and looked at each other. Then they smiled. Frank stood, and hurried to Ella. Debbie sat there, still smiling.

She told the story of a man. As soon as Frank entered the room, she stopped screaming and began to tell the story. He felt offended at first, but when he began to try to understand her story, despite its illogical telling, he felt less offended. Now and then, as she told the story, he watched her face, her body, and found that there was no trace of abnormality, and that she even smelled of Lux soap.

She told the story of a man bearing green wings. He was an angel, she said, a green angel. No, not green. An army-green angel. No, not army-green. "You know the color of an army uniform?" Frank said yes. She smiled. He was an angel that was the color of an army uniform. I did not hear what he said. But he spoke so well, so authoritatively. He said we cannot keep waiting for heaven. But we must look at the skies. Do you believe that heaven is nothing? The skies are here for us to see. Why must we look at heaven?" But, she said, the man could not fly. His wings failed him. He tried to. "Oh, how hard he tried. You see," she told Frank, "not all angels fly. Everyone can be an angel, but not everyone can fly. You doubt me because I can see skepticism in your eyes, let me tell you something I discovered. And this discovery is based on groundbreaking research, careful analysis. I am no sophist."

By this time Frank was listening raptly, finding some sequence, clues.

"Angels are of many colors. The prominent angels are white. Some black. Some green. Some army uniform color. I can only speak of these four. But specifically, I can speak of the angel of army uniform color. By the way, man is an angel. Every man is an angel. He might be white or black or of army uniform color. Tell me, what kind of angel are you?"

"I don't know," he said, and knew it was a mistake.

"You don't know!" she screamed, so that the silence that followed was deafening. He was accustomed to her screams by now. She said nothing further. He waited, probed her with his eyes, and matched her silence with his. She turned toward the window, facing it as though in meditation. Stationary, transfixed, an eternal sculpture, Ella said not another word. Her eyes were closed, so he waited, hoping she'd turn to him again and continue her story. She did not. He checked his wristwatch and recalled that he had a class to teach. He stood, glanced to see if she would turn to him, but she did not.

He left the room, offended.

XI

A week passed. In the morning he dressed for work, peeped into Debbie's room and saw that she was still sleeping. He heard a knock on the door. It was Goody. "I came to tell you I'm leaving for Abuja." She did not appear prepared for travel. She wore loose-fitting jeans and the red blouse she had worn when she had re-entered his life seven days ago. She had stayed in the city for the week to see that Ella's transition was comfortable. On her face he thought he could discern resignation, the absence of guts, hopelessness. He wore his pants without a belt, since they fit tightly; they were one of his old pairs: he had first worn them in his last year as an undergraduate. Goody was looking at his pants and the empty belt hooks; he felt ashamed. They were standing in front of the door, she staring at his waist and he thinking of what to say.

"Well," he said, finally, "You're leaving."

"I already said that." She turned and walked toward her car.

"Are you going to drive all the way?" he asked, still standing in front of the door.

"Sure. I drove all the way here."

"Oh. Right." He followed her and stood beside her. They rested their backs on the car and continued the silence they had begun earlier. This is *harmony*, Frank thought, and loved the way her thigh brushed against his. They were of the same height.

"There's some background to all this."

"Ella?"

"Yes."

"Okay."

"The past is not past."

"Faulkner?"

"Yes. All word is propaganda."

"Anthony Burgess."

She laughed and slapped his belly. It was what she would have done three years ago. "I'm scholarly," he said, laughing.

"I taught you. I taught you Faulkner and Burgess!" she teased.

"But you didn't teach me Shakespeare, at least."

"Oh yes. Nobody is taught Shakespeare," she said, laughing, slapping his belly again.

Then silence came and Frank continued to think it was harmony. Goody said, "Let's sit in the car."

He agreed, despite the fact he had to teach a class in five minutes. He decided to miss it. "What's this background?" he asked.

But she said, "Your face is wrinkling. You're only twenty-nine-years old. There's some discoloration on your nose. And I can't find the birthmark that used to be below your eyelid."

34

Then she added, "You still look like a Soviet man. Like a Nigerian Gorbachev. It makes your face curious. Fitzgerald should have written about you, not Benjamin Button."

She was being evasive, but he did not intrude. He let her find her path to what she wanted to say. He guessed it was something they had never talked about.

"There's some background to all this," Goody said, exhausting her descriptive powers.

"You said that before."

"Yes. Yes. I said that before." She looked out of the car window. Because Debbie's house was the last on the street and was surrounded by high shrubs, it was difficult to see passersby or the neighbor. He saw a man sitting on the ground, making marks on the ground with his hand. He recognized him. He mowed lawns and trimmed flowers for residents of the staff quarters. Frank turned and gazed directly at Goody. He saw that she had tears in her eyes.

"Goody," he said, touching her thigh.

"Ella is reacting to something from her childhood. She is reacting to our father."

Frank realized that she had scarcely spoken about him. He only knew that her father died during her first year in university.

"My father had sex with her. And me. He called us his angels. He never called us his daughters. Several times. He'd come to our room at night and lie between us, taking turns. I don't know why I am saying this."

"You don't have to say it."

"I've been silent about it. See, it has destroyed Ella. She was younger." Frank moved in his seat, stretching his hand, holding a part of her neck.

"It has not destroyed Ella."

"Our father used to say that he could teach us anything, even sex." She was smiling, and the tears coursing down her face seemed perfectly normal, as if she shed tears whenever she smiled.

"You don't have to talk about this."

"It's the background to where we are now."

"You've said enough."

"Okay. Okay." She bowed her head. His hand now held a part of her hair. It smelled of a relaxer cream, her usual brand. Her perfume was also present, a strong scent of apples.

"Goody."

"Yes. Yes," she said, still bowing her head. Her eyes were closed. "Stay here. Don't go. Deal with this."

"No," she said, opening her eyes forcefully. "I must go. Chris called yesterday."

"Chris called?"

"Yes. I can't leave him, Frank. I just can't."

"Oh. Right." He remembered when she had told him she was leaving him. He remembered he was wearing green corduroy pants, and that afterward he had felt stupid for being so under-dressed for her departure.

It took some time before Goody said, "I guess she slept with him."

"Who?"

"Abacha." The recently-deceased Head of State.

"Abacha?" Frank shook his head. He felt bare when he saw her looking at him with childlike candor.

"I'm not sure," she added.

"A dead man is a dead man. I can't even believe you're suggesting…"

"So what? So what, Frank?" she said, and opened the door. He opened his too. She turned and came to where he was. He had one leg still in the car. But she hugged him nonetheless. His arms stayed by his side, and his leg ached. She said, "Let me go, Frank. I'll call you." He nodded and stepped away from the car.

After she drove off, he saw that the man who mowed lawns and trimmed flowers was still bent, making marks on the ground. He seemed to be biding time. Frank felt he was biding time too.

XII

Before he knocked on Ella's door, he stopped at Debbie's room. She was still dressed in her pajamas, reading a journal. He did not knock before entering; this was a practice she had gotten used to. She said nothing. He was her only kin.

"I thought you had a class," she said, sitting up. "Yes. Goody came. I was already late."

"Goody." She looked at him and lowered her glasses, as though they made him foggy in her view. Her look told him much. He remembered Kate Chopin writing something about the past, which he disagreed with, but he quoted it to Debbie nonetheless. She read *The Awakening* every year.

"You remember what Chopin wrote?"

"What?"

"The past was nothing to her; offered no lesson which she was willing to heed," he quoted.

"Of course. Edna Pontellier." *The Awakening*'s protagonist.

"I hate that quote."

"There's nothing to hate"

This quieted him; he knew Goody had failed in her desire to forget the past.

Debbie's husband, Leke, had been a professor of philosophy, a scholar of Bertrand Russell, and Frank's teacher. But Frank remembered him more as a friend and mentor than as a teacher— Leke had supervised Frank's thesis at the graduate level, and had advised him to apply for a graduate assistant position in the Department of Philosophy. In Frank's memory, there were many things right, even righteous about Leke Craig. They included

37

his apolitical life. Their discussions ranged from critiques of texts published earlier that century—Russell's *Introduction to Mathematical Philosophy*, Ramsey's *The Foundations of Mathematics and Other Logical Essays*, and W.V. Quine's *The Philosophy of Logic*—to what was unimportant about military dictatorship. The works specifically stimulated Frank's interest in Leke, and in how he conducted his life. But up until the time he applied for the position of graduate assistant, he had never met Leke's wife—to whom Leke constantly referred as a plum sauce, a sort of Chinese seasoning for his life. The first time he talked of her in this manner, Frank said, "I'm impressed."

"About what?" Leke asked, tweaking his short goatee as was his practice. There was a smile on his face, the sort that resulted from a deep-seated happiness.

"The way you talk about your wife."

"She's my best asset." Frank, on hearing this, felt inclined to start an argument about a woman being an "asset"—why a woman couldn't and shouldn't be considered a commodity, a thing to be owned. But he weighed his options, especially because he believed Leke Craig was speaking sincerely, and maybe "asset" meant something different to him. Instead, and more usefully, he considered this a monumentality; few men could still refer to their wives as their best asset or as a plum sauce.

"I haven't met her," he said.

Leke stretched an arm across the table and slapped Frank's wrist. "You shouldn't feel bad about that. You've been a faithful boy, you know. You're a very loyal and faithful person. To everything. I've had fun with you, Frank. I swear to God! To introduce you to my wife would be an honor. She's just back from Ghana. Her sabbatical. You *deserve* to meet Debola."

"Those are kind words."

"Of course. We talk about you on the phone! You're a motif!"

Frank laughed, suddenly nervous, feeling whimsical. He looked around Leke's office—the books, falling atop each other on a ledge, the gift items from various countries Leke had visited, including a miniature wooden giraffe. "When can I come to the house?" He had never been to Leke's house. He realized that there was something in human interaction that could transcend physical abodes. Yet, it confused him when he tried to make logic of that thought.

"Tomorrow. She's expecting you. I swear to God, she's expecting you."

"You don't have to swear, Professor."

"I feel like I swear for a living."

Frank laughed. Then Leke slapped Frank's wrist again. Soon after, he tweaked his goatee. That was all that mattered at that moment to Frank. The goatee, to him, was his motif.

The day Debbie called and asked him to return from the University of Legon, where he was studying for his PhD at the time, he knew without being told that it had something to do with Leke. True, Leke belonged to a large family. But Debbie had once told him that she did not trust her husband's family, that once Frank had come into her husband's life, Frank had become his only family, in her view. This was about year after he had met her, a short time for their intimacy in Frank's thinking. She had made contacts with friends at the University of Legon in Accra, where she worked during her sabbatical year, and got him a post-graduate admission. But his love for Leke had ended his studies. It was a sacrifice Frank was willing to make.

"It's important, Frank," Debbie said. "Come back."

"When?" Frank asked, trying to gauge her seriousness.

"Today. Now."

"Why?"

"I can't say on the phone."

"Is it about Leke?"

What made him catch a flight the next morning was her voice, the fact that it gave away nothing. When he entered the house she was dressed only in a nightgown, sitting on the living room floor. The room was half-filled with men, all of whom were sitting on the furniture. Frank did not know many of them. He stood beside the door, not daring to sit. He recognized Dr. Samanja, who was Leke's closest colleague. Frank had the passing thought that, if he had not traveled for his PhD, *he* would have been Leke's closest colleague. When Debbie looked at him, glancing over as though he was a shadow, as though it was not his face that she looked at, he knew something had happened, something vaguely sketchy. Just as he was about to ask about Leke, Debbie stood and said, "Tell them, Frank. We can't bury him in Ekiti. It's here. Here." The men suddenly had a presence, as though they were brought to life by Debbie's words.

Frank asked, looking at the men now, scanning their faces for disapproval, "Leke? You're talking about Leke?"

One of the men, wearing a threadbare ankara shirt and accompanying trousers, said, "Madam. He is our brother. We will decide where to bury him." Then another man said something in Yoruba Frank did not understand. Debbie, still standing, said, "Say something, Frank. You're my only kin. They cannot take him away from me." After she said this, she moved backward, rested her back on the wall, and slid back to the floor. Even from where she sat beside the door, she seemed in control. The men, as Frank saw them, were reluctant pawns, gladiatorial combatants who were neither cheering nor fighting.

Frank said nothing. He could not. He wanted to speak out and say something significant, something apt in Debbie's defense. Perhaps if he said something meaningful, he could be quoted, the men would go away thinking that his wisdom had outwitted them. But he could not. It was too sudden to think; death had mesmerized him. When no one spoke again, the man in threadbare ankara stood up, glanced at Debbie, and in seeming to take a swipe at her with this action, walked toward the door. He locked eyes with Frank. The man's pleading look did not persist. After a few seconds, he was out of the living room, his feet making a scampering sound. Debbie occupied Frank's thoughts, so he turned to her. She stood from the floor, gingerly, as though performing a rite. She said, looking at all the other men, including Dr. Samanja, "Please, leave. Leave my house." The men shuffled their feet, whispered among themselves, but did not really hesitate. Of course Frank could not tell how many times they had visited. Yet, from the way they sprang to their feet, it appeared that telling them to leave was simply a natural consequence of their meetings with Debbie. Furthermore, it appeared that they had only launched an offense against Debbie to test their powers. Apparently, that test had failed.

"Dr. Samanja, please. I want to be alone." Frank, confused at what Debbie wanted, followed Dr. Samanja. Debbie said, "I didn't ask you to leave, Frank. Stay here, please. Stay with me."

The following days were cloudy in his memory. But the days did pass. The burial was perfunctory. He feared Debbie would lose her mind, or *something*, but by all indications she didn't, so he couldn't point to her grieving pattern. She didn't shout; there were no graveside hysterics. He, not she, poured the sand. She stayed in a different room—having moved few of her things from the room she had shared with Leke. She said to Frank, "I can't share a room with his things. At least not now."

Frank attended to every visitor; most knew he had been close to Leke. The Vice Chancellor insisted, saying in his thin, wry voice, "I want to see Professor Debola."

"You can't see her, Sir," Frank replied, polite but firm. When he was alone again, he went to Debbie and stated, "I can't cover for you. You have to do what you have to do, for yourself."

Debbie said nothing. She sat writing on a white sheet of paper, clumsily, writing each letter of each word in bold. It was her Inaugural Lecture, scheduled for a month after Leke's. She'd refused to change the date. Frank walked away from the room, annoyed at the way she was grieving. He could not figure it out, name it, or even ascribe precision to it. There were times, like then, when he felt that everything should have mathematical precision—so he could assign numerical values to mourning, find an almighty formula for solving emotional distresses. Times, like then, when he felt helplessly overshadowed by trauma and began to think that one could not solve life with algebra.

Frank did not return to Ghana. Debbie did not ask him to stay or to live with her. Yet, the day after the burial, he went to a storage facility outside the university and gathered his things. Frank moved into Debbie's house, which had been Leke's too, and took residence in the room beside hers.

XIII

Debbie said—that morning when he stopped in her room after Goody visited, on his way to knock on Ella's door—"I sometimes feel I can't let go. My body wants to walk, but my mind is here. I want to forget. It's been a year." He felt the need to hold her shoulders, but didn't. She noticed the movement of his hands. She said, "Feel my shoulders."

"What?" he asked.

"See how strong my wings are."

He laughed loud, but uncomfortably.

"Come on, Frank. I'm serious." So he did as she asked. But his fingers pressing down her shoulders felt too weak to him.

He wondered if he had done it properly, the wing-checking. Her eyes were closed when he touched her shoulders, so he wasn't sure. Debbie, eyes still closed, his fingers lightly touching her, said, "I always remember Mademoiselle Reisz in Chopin's book. She said something about how strong Edna's wings should be, and how those without strong wings end up on the floor, fallen from the sky. I think about my wings all the time. I ask myself if I am ready to fly."

"You're not ready, Debbie." She opened her eyes when Frank said this. For his part, Frank did not understand himself, why he said she wasn't ready to fly. He began to think, as he avoided her questioning gaze, that she was contemplating suicide. If he could covertly dissuade her, he would save her. In some way, especially in the light of her wing theory, he considered himself a mercy-giver. He must look upon her with mercy and redeem her. She said, "Call Abigail for me." Abigail was the housemaid. He did not glance at Debbie as he walked out.

He stood before Ella's door and called out to Abigail. When she answered, he shouted that it was Debbie who wanted her, then he knocked on Ella's door. A gush of cold wind ran through his mind, something he'd never experienced before. It was not fear he suddenly felt; it was the feeling of a coming realization, the feeling archangels get when the trumpet is about to sound.

As before, his arrival awakened Ella. She sat up on the bed as soon as he entered; beside her was an open book. Her duffel bag, packed for her by Goody, was open with clothes spilling out. It was the first time in the ten days she had been there that she was changing her clothes. It wasn't a sign to Frank. It was an occurrence. He didn't want to believe in signs, especially not in any sign that would suggest deliverance, change, or anything good for that matter. The room was otherwise in good shape. He saw something new, though: a candelabrum. He made a mental note to find a candle for it. When he summoned courage to glance at Ella, he noticed her tightly packed hair, and noticed that she again smelled of Lux. It was a scent that indulged him to believe she did not need him. She began to speak, reciting something:

> Garlic and sapphires in the mud
> Clot the bedded axle-tree.
> The trilling wire in the blood
> Sings below inveterate scars
> Appeasing long forgotten wars.

He didn't know whose lines they were. Now sitting beside Ella, and all the more aware of the agreeableness of her Lux-odor, he supposed she could not have composed something that intelligible. He asked her, "Who wrote that?" She looked at him and smiled engagingly, drawing him into her charm. Frank saw it as her newly possessed wiles. He believed he had never seen her so beautiful. Even her bushy, unlined eyebrows seemed perfect. Still smiling, she said, "I guess it was Eliot. The first of his four quartets. He read it to me."

"Who?"

"Why do you want to know?" All the while Ella smiled. He even dared to smile back, but she didn't find his smile entertaining. "It's none of your business."

"Oh, right," Frank said.

"Of course. Right, trite. Fight."

"What?"

"What sounds like the first syllable for water. Like fought."

"Yes," Frank said, hoping she'd find nothing to say against "yes."

"They say yes all the time. Yes sir. You should never say no to your superior. It's almost like a death sentence. You say no, you say no to life. You understand me?" Frank said yes, and recalled his last conversation with her about angels and their colors.

44

She asked him, "What do you know about life?"

"What?"

"Do you answer every question with 'What,' or 'Oh, right'?"

"Oh. Sorry."

She laughed now at his "sorry." For the first time he felt ashamed beside Ella; she appeared to have overpowered him, to have clearly outplayed him in guts and in brains. She grew serious. All the light in her face disappeared. He became instantly paranoid, could not understand how it was that Ella was in charge of *his* situation. His paranoia was a response to her seriousness. Her switching off her smile triggered dark feelings within him. One thought led to another, one feeling tangled with others, and before long he was remembering his father's photograph, in black and white, faint and blurry. Frank's father was already dead when he was born. Frank then remembered Leke. There were times, such as the present moment sitting beside Ella, when Leke's death forcibly became apparent and lost its usual haziness. In those moments, he saw or imagined how Leke was shot. His memory painted a picture of Leke stepping out of his car; he must have been confused at all the noise around him, all the people with green branches, all the parked cars that forced him to pull over. He imagined how, when the first shot rang, Leke must have tried to enter his car but failed, given the number of people who had gathered around him, begging to be let into his car. Leke might not have seen the soldiers or even understood why they were around in the first place. Being apolitical, he could not have known there was an anti-Abacha protest in Ibadan opposite the Lekan Salami Stadium, where he had parked. There was a second shot, which must have sounded close to Leke, and when he began to feel pain in his neck, he might have held his neck, saying something like "Damn" or "Shit" or addressing some curse to no one in particular. If he knew he was dying, he might have thought of Debola, his plum sauce, or some of the good times they'd enjoyed together.

"You must listen to me," Ella said, calling him from his imagined memory.

"Yes. Yes."

"Why did he die?" she said.

"Who?"

She stood and screamed, "You can't keep asking me who! You must know him! You must know him!"

"I'm sorry," he said, really overcome with guilt.

She sat again, then held his left hand with both hers. She smiled.

"Give me eggs," she said, entreatingly, "and some milk. I want to have an egg milkshake."

"What?"

"Give me eggs," she repeated, before adding a shout, "Give me eggs!"

In response, he shouted as she had done, "Abigail!" When Abigail came, Frank described what he conjured as an egg milkshake. "Put two eggs in a cup, stir it, and add a tin of milk then bring it. Fast, Abigail." The girl stood there, watching him. She was clearly stupefied.

"Do as he says, Abigail!" Ella suddenly commanded. The maid turned, and Frank heard her walk the hallway in slow, unsure steps.

"She's bringing it," Frank said to Ella, to whom he felt enslaved.

"Yes. Thank you. He did it."

Having learned not to ask who, he simply said, "Yes."

"It's a beautiful thing. You should try it. Egg milkshake. Wonderful. Wonderful." He could have asked her if she had ever tried it, but he wasn't sure what she wanted to be asked, or what questions would infuriate her. Soon, he heard footsteps; it was

Abigail coming to announce that there were no more eggs in the kitchen.

He heard Debbie's laughter. Ella now started screaming, "Give me egg milkshake!" Frank felt like hitting her. She seemed too much like a pampered child, or a pampered goddess; he didn't know what else to think she was. But he remained beside her, enduring her screams, wanting to leave.

XIV

Each time he wanted to stand, Ella pulled him close, urging him to stay. She had dispensed with her demand for a milkshake as soon as evening arrived, when the sun's rays were still filtering into the room. Frank sat with her for hours; there wasn't a clock in the room. The day, which began with his conversations with Goody, then Debbie, then Ella, appeared endless. Yet, despite the cramps he felt from sitting in the same position for a long time, and still wearing shoes, he had no desire other than to sit beside Ella, with her resting her head on his shoulder and her hand grasping his.

She fell asleep. At that moment, Debbie's car started up and he heard it pull away. It was the last thing he remembered, for he too fell asleep. He created expressive art with Ella. In their sleeping position they could have been sculpted into a masterpiece. If Frank had had the capacity to stay awake while asleep and to view their position, he might have remembered what Debbie said on the afternoon he told her about Ella's problem—that Ella had returned because she was in love with him.

She woke up with a shout. And like a nanny, Frank woke too. "Can't you hear his voice? He's talking," she said, looking around the room for a face that matched the voice she was hearing. Frank remained wordless, as perturbed by her sudden shout and words as by his impromptu awakening.

"Listen to what he's saying. Listen. *This regime will be firm, humane, and decisive. It will not condone or tolerate any act of indiscipline. Any attempt to test our will shall be decisively dealt with. This government is a child of necessity.* Did you hear him?"

Frank said "Yes," and it sounded believable. Just then he heard Debbie's car drive in—there was a sharp squeaking noise when she braked. He knew the brake oil was depleted. He made a mental note to call a mechanic the next day.

"His voice had a good feeling. I loved to listen to it. It sounded better when he was with me. The radio and television tell a lie. Don't believe whatever they say. Do you hear me?"

"Yes," said Frank, once again the pupil, receiving lessons about living.

"You know, he came every day. It was a new world. A small house. Everything. Everything was mine. Sometimes he'd ask me to untie his boots or shoes."

Frank remembered what Goody had said about Ella and Abacha. He shook his head.

"You think I'm lying?"

"No."

"I'm lying?"

"No."

"I was not afraid. All the things I heard about him. He told me I was a good woman. He told me he needed me. He was having difficult times. No, not difficult. He couldn't have used that word. I think he said something about pressure. Did he say pressured times?" Frank, not realizing the question had been directed at him, looked at her keenly, even with accusation. His disbelief was scattering. By now she had placed her head on his shoulder again. "Did he use that word? Pressure?"

He could have said "I don't know" but those words seemed unacceptable.

"I think he did. He was under a lot of pressure. Sure."

"Yes. Sure. He once talked about the Boys Brigade. He liked their motto: Sure and Steadfast. Are you wearing shoes?"

"Oh. Yes. Yes."

"Let me show you how I usually removed his shoes." She bent and untied his shoes, one by one, expertly. Then she pulled the right shoe and drew it to her face, sniffing it. "It doesn't smell like his. You are fake."

"I am not him. I can't be *him*," Frank retorted, offended that she even voiced the thought that he could be *him*, especially because everything pointed to a him no one wanted to be like.

"Do you even know who he was? You sound like a hater. You hate everything. When you start to hate, everything dies off. You know that?"

"Well, yes." He decided to consider her normal; all she was saying was too reasonable to be dismissed as the ranting of a half-sane person. He felt he was being admitted to therapy, Ella being his therapist.

"You know you're a hater?" Ella asked.

"I am not a hater."

"You are."

"I am not."

"You are."

"Why do you say that?"

"Everyone who hates him is a hater. It doesn't matter what he did."

"I am not a hater."

"You are a hater!"

He stood without looking at her and left the room. He bumped into Debbie, who had been standing in front of the door. She had certainly been eavesdropping. "Get back inside, Frank," she demanded. But he ignored her. Ella offended him; she called him a hater. He took Debbie's car keys, checking the time and seeing it was half past seven. The mechanic could still attend to him. He felt that he was like that car. His brakes needed oiling, and his life too.

Goody called Frank a day later. When the phone rang it sounded like his life chiming. He had not gone in to see Ella again; he still felt offended. But his heart skipped a beat when he heard Abigail open the door to Ella's room. Even Debbie, who more and more stayed home instead of going to the university, didn't go in there. And so more and more he was providing for the house. The experience was new; he had always depended on Debbie for support. He was sure she was paid, given her status, but thought that, for whatever reason, she had become too lazy to spend money.

So, with his life chiming like the telephone and his consciousness calcifying into something he could not figure, he took the call. It came with a screech—the connection was poor. When the sound improved, he recognized Goody's voice. As always, it recalled his life and summoned the past. Something obvious leaped from the telephone: *She was his memory.*

"Can you hear me?"

"Of course."

There was no doubt she heard the offense in his voice and the arsenal of anger behind it. "You're angry with me?"

"You are keeping things from me. You are making a fool of me."

"Is this…is this something from Ella?"

"You're keeping things from me." He heard her laughter. Then a sniff. "I don't care what happened, Goody. I don't even care about you or Ella. I just need to know. I need to know. I don't care if I do nothing with the knowledge of what happened. It's a plain desire, simple."

"Simple? Is that what you think this is? Plain and simple?"

"If I know nothing of what *this* is, how can I appropriately call it good, or bad? It's crazy. What do you make of me? A fool? A hater?"

"I don't know what you are. I don't know what anybody is."

Then, dropping his weapon, he said, "Tell me what happened to Ella."

Her voice, as she spoke of ignorance, of knowing no one, sounded desperate, an avalanche of trauma. "I only know what my husband told me."

"Your husband?"

"Yes. Chris told me. He took her to Abacha. She stayed one week in a chalet. The first three days, he visited only once. But after the third day, he got close to her, liked her, and spent more time with her. That is all I know."

"All? Is that all, Goody?"

"My name is Goodness, Frank. Not Goody." She laughed, and he could hear her nervousness, her restraint.

"There is something more, Goodness." He was firm. She relented.

"Yes. She was with him the night he died. I think so. Even Chris was not sure. When the news filtered in that he had died, and everyone wasn't sure, and everyone was caught off guard, Ella looked calm. Chris found her sitting on the floor in the long hallway that led to the chalet. She said nothing to him. He spoke and she listened, and obeyed, and followed him home."

Frank sighed. Goody sighed. But when he heard her sniffle loudly, his belly tightened and he wasn't sure why. There was a long silence. Frank began to feel indebted to Goody, even to Ella. He felt he owed an obligation to all those who told their lives to him. And now he could not ascertain whether he could keep their lives to himself, hold them close, and avoid a fall. He knew how difficult it was going to be—handling all the details of Ella, Goody, Debbie, his mother, Leke…It was an unending list. But he wanted to try. It would not matter if he failed. It wouldn't matter even if by trying he was setting himself up to fail. Perhaps he was a point of contact or a hub. He was a man with a severe onset of troubles from more lives than he could fathom. But as with everything else that came from Goody, he wasn't sure.

The line went dead. He couldn't tell if it Goody had hung up or the call had been dropped. Uncertainty was a known oblivion.

XV

There was no hate in him anymore; all of it dissipated with Goody's call. The hate he felt for Ella was replaced with a consuming desire to know everything. So, immediately after Goody's call, he walked to Ella's room. He could hear her singing a song he did not know. But because the lines were simple, two lines which she repeated over and over, he soon learned the words; the music seemed to be coming from far away.

I've got you under my skin
I've got you deep in this heart of mine

Ella sang on, even when he entered. She lay on her belly, legs raised to form a ninety-degree angle to her torso. Frank felt like straightening her limbs, but he did not dare. She was at peace and he didn't want to intrude. He felt that it would be best to walk away from the room and leave her alone. She stopped after she sang the song two more times. Even when she said, "I had only one boyfriend before him," it sounded like part of her song.

Frank sat on the bed. Her legs were still raised. He couldn't guess what was right for him to ask. She would lead him, he would follow, or else he wasn't sure. Yet, the words spilled from his mouth, "He was your boyfriend?"

She turned abruptly, suddenly sitting up on the bed, a wide grin on her face. She said, "He was more than my boyfriend."

Frank asked, "He was? He was a good man?"

Ella's smile disappeared slowly, like the coming of dusk. "He was a good man, at first. He hid things from me. Then he began to tell me of all the things he did. All the things he wanted to do."

It would be a mistake to ask her what he had told her. But who was he? Frank needed her to unmask the man; he needed an escape from pronouns. But, as pressing as these needs were, he could not find the right question; with Ella he had to be careful.

"He did not touch me until I asked him to. It's difficult to meet him and refuse him. I mean, it's difficult to know who he was and say to yourself later that you were with him in a room alone and you did nothing with him. It is a crime. I would blame myself forever. I seized every opportunity. I waited for him naked." She said this with a shy smile, sly even, as though roles were being swapped and Frank was the man she talked about.

"It reminds me of the first night he came. He looked at me and said I was not beautiful. I was something other than beauty. You can hear him speak these words with certainty; they did not sound foreign. He wanted to talk to me. He felt he was being misunderstood, and he did not like that. He wanted to be humane, but decisive. His greatest weakness was to be considered weak. He said there's nothing worse than being considered weak. It's okay if you're considered inhumane, if they call you a dictator. But it's never forgivable if you're considered weak. You understand me?"

Frank asked, "Who is a good man? You say he was a good man." He came close to asking who he was. His heart pounded.

53

"You have to stop asking me questions. I want to talk. I want you to listen to me."

"I am sorry."

"Yes, good. Good like he touched me, took me in his arms. I was naked but he took me in his arms and I felt like I was clothed. The first day he came in and saw the way I was, on the bed covered only with the blanket, he said nothing. He touched me. He touched me. I want you to listen to me."

She sounded monotonous, so he said, "I am listening to you."

"You must listen to me. That is what he told me." She quieted for a moment.

"Would you listen to me? If I said something?" Frank asked, taking advantage of her silence, of her eyes looking at something in the distance only she could see.

"No. I wouldn't. I wouldn't listen to you speak of something you know nothing about."

"I know nothing?"

"Have you heard a man speak of death as if dying is living? The telephone is ringing. It is the fourth day. He has just touched me. He is saying something about termination, take them out, all of them, not one of them should come out. I knew he was speaking of death, but he said it as if he was giving life. I don't know how he could speak of death as if it was life."

"What did you do?"

"I told him he could never touch me again."

"And what did he say?"

"He laughed. He wore his uniform. It was rumpled. I didn't care. I had pulled it off him. I didn't care. I told him I had a right to do with myself what I wanted to do. And when he left me, he was laughing. He thought I was joking." By now, there was a quality of assertive stillness in her face. She appeared like a legendary griot, one who told stories of the past in a way that made them stories of the present.

"But he came back on the fifth day. I did not allow him to touch me. I told him to his face that he was a killer. I told him to his face that I could kill him and save others the stress. But he laughed, called me a woman. He said I was like every woman. I was too weak. I was a fool. The surprising thing was that he didn't shout at me. He said it too quietly. I was prepared for a fight. I could have been killed. I could have been killed for calling him a killer. But I didn't care. He had touched me so much and killed so much that I didn't care if I died or if he killed again. I didn't want him to touch me again. It was plain and simple."

"It was the fifth day?"

"Yes. All the while I was a fool."

Frank said nothing. There was nothing he could say, or ask. Things were becoming clear.

"He didn't touch me again after that."

Because he felt that things were becoming clear, and she'd trusted him with many details, he said, "I want you to tell me if he died or not. What happened to him?"

She slapped him. She lay down again, her belly on the bed, her legs raised up, as she had been when he had entered. But as he rubbed his cheek, she brought them down and began singing again. It was the same song. Frank knew she would not speak to him again. He stood up and cursed her under his breath, but felt relieved.

XVI

Mrs. Anjola had a face that varied. It could seem corpulent one instant, then look like it lacked flesh the next. Frank knew this; he ascribed that quality to her the first day they met. On the morning of Ella's tenth day in Debbie's house when she knocked on the door, he determined that Mrs. Anjola's face had changed into the one without flesh. She wore a t-shirt that outlined her body. Never before had Frank considered her small. She seemed the opposite of what she was like when she said no to Frank *and* Goody, disapproving of their union. She was corpulent then, full of the awareness that she wielded dormant power.

"Good morning, Ma."

"Frank," she said, unsure of whether she wanted to enter the house.

"Come in. You want to see Ella?"

She said nothing until she was inside. "I don't know. How is she?"

"Sit down, Ma." When she sat, looking at him pleadingly, Frank suddenly became aware of how much her daughters looked like her. Goody resembled her in warfare, while Ella inherited her sense of void.

"She's fine. She's been talking to me."

"Thank God. I pray for her every day. It is a bad thing to happen to a mother."

"Yes, Ma. But she is fine. She will be fine."

"You must tell me the truth. I have not come here for lies. Lies can kill all of us."

"Yes." He wouldn't look at her. She was still the woman he knew to be overflowing with disgust, the flooded Nile in orbit. If he looked at her, he would think too much of the past, he would recall memories destined to be shut away. And it might affect his relationship with Ella, now that they had something going.

"I cannot lie to you, Ma. I cannot."

"Yes. She called your name. She trusts you."

She was a mixture of warfare and void; she could shoot a gun with one hand and paint with another.

"You want to see her?"

"Who?"

"Ella."

"Oh. It's useless. I would make a fool of myself."

Frank knew it would be right to prod her, but he thought it would make no difference. "I am sorry about what happened to her."

"I don't know what happened to her. Goody is keeping it from me."

He hoped she would not ask him. He cautioned himself; he had said too much. It was her presence, his desire to say the correct thing that made him talkative.

"God bless you, Frank. You are doing too much for me."

He felt relieved; he added her to his list of persons for whom his life counted. Perhaps his only reason for existence was to help the Anjola family? They were his life's purpose. But he wasn't sure he could achieve that end.

"I wanted to come and say thank you."

"Okay. Okay," he nodded.

"You need anything?"

"No. No. I am fine."

Mrs. Anjola stood. She looked happy. "You're sure you don't want to see her?"

"I will make a fool of myself. I cannot see her. You say she's fine."

"Yes. She's fine."

"Has she said anything about me?"

"No. She has not."

Mrs. Anjola made to move, then hesitated. There were too many unfinished matters. Frank did not know why, but he looked at her handbag. It was worn. She might have used it for a decade. It seemed familiar.

She said, "You know, I remember when Ella had just entered the university. We went out together. We went to the market.

There was a soldier whipping a man. You know how they flog. When Ella saw him she went to him and told him to stop. Her voice was small. There was a crowd. The man who was being flogged had probably stolen, or maybe he had done nothing. You know how these people do things because they can do things. Ella told him to stop. She did not fear him. And he looked at her. I thought he was going to flog her too. But he stopped. Then he smiled at Ella."

Frank felt overcome by an emotion he could not identify. Mrs. Anjola continued, "I don't know Ella. I have wanted to know her all her life. Sometimes I feel she is not my daughter. She is too far away. You see, I am talking too much." She stepped toward Frank, placed her hands on both of his shoulders, and said, "Thank you. You are doing too much for me."

XVII

Mrs. Anjola's visit, and the weight of indescribable emotion he felt afterward, readied Frank for Goody's call. When he held the receiver, it felt heavy, but when he put it to his ear and heard Goody's voice, it felt light. The line was clear. The weightlessness of her voice and the clarity of the line made him feel good.

"Your mum came to the house."

"*The* house? I guess it's not your house..."

He heard her chuckle. He said, "You're stupid." She chuckled more. There was a gush of warm air in his left ear. He felt happy. But he feared he'd lose it any moment.

"What did she say? She came to see Ella?"

"No. She came to see me."

"You?"

"Yes."

"That's out of place. She didn't see Ella?"

"I asked her to see Ella. She refused."

58

After a pause Goody intoned, "I miss her. I miss my mother." She added, "I wish I was more like her. She takes everything in, like a sponge. She's a sponge. I feel like I am a basket." She chuckled.

To Frank her chuckle sounded like a whimper. He felt sorry for her. Yet, as much as he tried, he couldn't find the parameters of his pity. "You did not tell your mum what happened to Ella."

"You're accusing me?"

"I'm asking you."

"That's not the tone for questions. You're worthy of hate."

"Ha ha. Very funny."

"I'm serious, Frank. I called you. And you insult me?"

She sounded different. Frank figured she was ready to fight. It was unusual of him, but he decided to square up to her.

"This is crazy stuff you're saying, Ella."

"I'm not Ella. My name is Goodness."

"I don't care what your name is. You are holding back from all of us what happened to your sister. She speaks of a man, someone in the Army. You know who the man is. It's up to you to be fair to all of us."

"I guess you're part of the 'us' you talk about. I don't know you as 'us.' You're not part of anything. You're just Frank."

"Oh, right. I'm just Frank. Fine. Yet you begged me to help your sister. Isn't that very wrong? Isn't it wrong?"

"Shut up, Frank." Then she began to sob. But Frank was not pacified.

"You'll answer my question! You can cry from now till next year. It does not matter. Who was the man Ella went to?"

"I told you. I told you Chris took her to Abacha."

Her voice—the appealing way in which she spoke—unnerved him. "I am sorry." She did not respond, so he pressed. "Goody? I am really sorry. I was caught off guard. You made me angry."

"Oh, yes. You made me angry too. I don't know why I was angry. I am far away but I am in this. I don't know what happened to Ella. I feel sorry. I feel guilty, Frank."

"It was Abacha? I guessed it was him."

"We're all guessing. Perhaps all this is a guess."

Then Frank remembered Ella saying she did not let the man touch her. "The last time I spoke with Ella, she said she did not let him touch her."

"She said so?"

Frank could hear hope in her voice, a switch of mood. "Well, as a matter of fact, he *touched* her. But after she heard him on the telephone giving orders to kill, she did not let him touch her anymore."

"I don't know what to say."

"Oh, right."

"I guess Ella is teaching us. All of us." She chuckled. Frank took her words seriously.

"You're right, Goody. It's a matter of fact." He became introspective and worried that it had spoiled the conversation.

He guessed Goody figured that too, because she said, "Let me go. I will call you later."

"No. I should call you. I'll call you."

"Well, bye."

"Bye." He felt another gush of warm air in his ear.

XVIII

He would fail to remember what Ella had looked like at that moment. He would only remember the fabric with the poorly drawn swastika—and her voice. Her voice sounded incipient. But this incipience made her sound more real than she had ever sounded. Frank would curse himself; she had given too many signs, and clues. Yet he had remained unaware.

Her first words, when he entered her room and saw her standing with her arms folded, were, "You remember Wittgenstein?"

"Of course," he replied, smiling. She remembered her days as a philosophy student. When he looked above her, he saw the poorly drawn swastika. He checked his wristwatch. It was 2:00 p.m.

"I remembered him today. There was no logic in his death. You think you know about logic? You think there is some order about everything? You must be silent about what you cannot speak about. Wittgenstein couldn't have explained this. Could he have explained to me what made him fall? He showed me a gun. He told me that killing me would be easy. He is holding a gun and he is undressing me. Then he pushes me to the bed. I am naked. I close my eyes but I can hear him undressing. Then I feel his body on mine. Then he is limp. He is limp. I open my eyes and find saliva on his mouth. That is it. That is all I know. I swear. I don't know anything else."

Frank felt his heart in his mouth. It would've been better if another person had told him this, if it had been hearsay. The narration by a third party would have lessened the weight. He sat on the bed and covered his head with his hands. He heard Goody saying *I guess Ella is teaching us,* but it sounded too true to be true. He might have believed it if she had told him again.

Ella sat beside him. She said, "Frank."

He asked her, "Is it Abacha?"

"Abacha?"

"Yes."

"I don't know," she said

He surprised himself. He held her shoulders and shook her violently. He saw the surprise in her eyes, but he kept shaking her—like a mad man.

"You must tell me!"

"Yes! Yes!" Ella screamed.

But he did not feel gratified. He felt she owed him much more. He kept shaking her shoulders though the madness had gone out of his effort. He heard her crying, the sound of a door opening, the sound of Debbie's footsteps. At that moment he heard all the noise possible, all the words that had been exchanged between Ella and him, all her screams and rants.

Ella did not resist. She let him shake her shoulders. When he finally felt gratified, when he started to feel silly, he stopped. Ella hugged him tight. Debbie watched all that happened. He hugged the girl in return. Ella kept crying. He did not know why, but he began to laugh. At first it was a mild cackle then it became full-bodied. But it was not infectious. Ella did not join him. She continued crying. He did not hear when Debbie left the room.

XIX

When he woke the next morning from a sleep filled with euphoric dreams of Ella's recovery, he walked into Debbie's room without knocking, as usual. He was eager to talk with her. She was lying on her back—her hands folded atop her stomach.

"Debbie," he said. He moved to the bed and sat beside her, placing his hands on hers, thinking that she meant more to him than his mother, and that it wouldn't be immoral to conclude this.

"Have you checked Ella? I think she's gone."

I think she's gone rang in his ears. Even Debbie's voice sounded ethereal; no ether could have a calming effect on her.

"Are you okay? Ella's better. Are you alright?"

"Ella's better? You think so? You think there's an end to this?"

"Are you okay, Debbie?"

"My wings have disappeared. I'm falling."

"That's not a correct thing to say. You are fine. You're standing."

She chuckled, but it could've easily been a whimper, or a distress call. "I have deceived you for too long. This is a rat race. Ella is a rat race. It will not end."

"I don't understand you, Debbie. You're talking too much."

"I should have told you this a long time ago."

"What?"

"I have no wings. I am falling."

Frank shook his head. Surprisingly, her eyes remained closed. There was a jerk in his arms. He constrained himself from forcing her eyes open.

"Debbie. You're not fine."

"Go and check Ella. I think she's gone."

I think she's gone rang again in his ears. He could not tell when he got up, or when he moved to Ella's room. He could not tell when he knocked, entered the room, or saw the bed neatly made and Ella's bag gone. He called Debbie from Ella's room twice. His words did not sound as if they left his mouth; they were muffled. As a matter of fact, he felt muffled. The moment would extend into the coming months—*I think she's gone.*

The only thing left to do was to remember.

TWO

ONE MAN

I

Face washing

My life at that time was comprised of several face-washings. It was because of my nervousness, my heart's refusal to be steady, my fear, the voices speaking gloom, and the imminent demise that I contemplated. In those days I listened to the radio, mostly the news, but often I allowed myself the luxury of the musical interludes, the advertisements, obituary announcements, town hall meetings, and political campaigns. Each evening after I listened to the news, especially on the evenings before the election results were announced, I went into the bathroom and washed my face. This became a graceless ritual, something I did without knowing what I was doing, perhaps only to look at my wet face in the mirror, perhaps nothing more but an activity to pass time.

I liked to think, then, that I could articulate the mood of Jos with the music that played after the news. Often the music that followed was Jim Reeves' "I'll Fly Away," especially because it was mostly obituaries that were announced after the day's news. Yet on the evening when the election results were announced no music followed. Not even Reeves' song was played, just a quirky silence, an empty voicelessness, as though the radio station could not transmit any further. I thought I was attributing too much to this intransmittability, this absence of music, and I understood why I considered myself logic-resistant. I was the kind of person who put two things together that were mutually exclusive, simply for the sake of having them together.

When I heard the election results, I stood from the loveseat I usually sat on, looked over the page of the book I was reading, and walked to the bathroom to wash my face. While rinsing I caught a glance of myself in the mirror, and I remember thinking that it would have been perfect if I was one-eyed, not blind, but one-eyed, so that I could see less completely. But that thought was completely unrelated to the present circumstances.

I knew that the announcement of the results was a marker, a pointer of some sort. It was one of those things I could know without being told, like smelling the sea from a distance or hearing the sound of a party from an unidentifiable house.

I walked out of the bathroom, took a flashlight I usually kept in the sitting room, and headed for the church. Living in a rectory was one of the things that unsettled me—it meant I lived on the threshold of righteousness, sinlessness, but I doubt that I would be able to manage or even attempt such a life. Everything in my life up to that point had been circumstantially premised, so that I often found myself doing things and being in situations in which I had no hand.

I did not expect anyone in the church, but I found that one of its doors was ajar—it was quite dark. Earlier in the evening there had been a power cut, and it was the time of the year when the day easily became night. I pointed the flashlight into the church because I heard murmurs. I recognized one of the voices easily— Joshua, the sexton.

"Joshua," I called.

"Yes sir," he answered, and I heard footsteps approaching the door. He was guided by my light. It seemed he had been there for quite some time, perhaps before nightfall.

"Who's there with you?"

"My brother, sir."

I became pensive; Joshua had never talked about his brother.

"What's he doing here?"

Joshua said nothing. By now he was almost at the door, and I could hear his brother moving toward me as well. I pointed the light directly at Joshua's face, and saw that his eyes gleamed with tears. He must have been crying. He stood facing me, and now his eyes were streaming with tears. When his brother approached I saw that he was crying too.

And I remember thinking that maybe before I came they were crying to God in prayer, some request that couldn't be answered except with tears, for weeping made God understand the sentimental value of their need.

Their crying ended quickly. An embarrassing silence followed. I think they felt ashamed of showing their emotions in front of me. I did not think their tears were unnecessary. I only wondered what was happening, what had happened. Something in the way they cried reminded me of the lack of music after the election results were announced. To end the silence, and their embarrassment, I said, "Tell me what happened."

At that moment there was a sudden noise from the gate, a number of people seemed to be knocking at the same time. I looked at Joshua but he looked at his brother. The gate was about a hundred yards away. Because my flashlight was still pointed at Joshua, just below his chin, I could see the fear in his eyes, which I admit began to seep into my head; it was like an ink stain on a white shirt, obvious. His brother was also afraid, and I couldn't tell if it was Joshua who infected him or if it was the other way around.

Joshua stepped out from the church and called, "Who's there?" There was a distant call of "Reverend!"

We didn't even need to exchange glances. Joshua moved in front, I fell in behind him; his brother followed. We marched to the gate, and while I walked I considered that the only response I could give to a strange voice that called for me was to listen to that voice, meet the stranger. When we got to the gate, the voices weren't one but many, all of them saying, "Reverend!" Our footsteps must have readied them for our coming, but it was "Reverend!" they called; it was me they wanted. But this quickly changed.

"Who's here?" Joshua asked. I noticed his hand held the bolt of the gate, ready to unlatch.

"Joshua!" a female voice moaned. The voice was deflated.

"Ma!" Joshua replied. His brother called out.

Joshua swung open the gate. A woman stepped into the church compound, but she was not alone. Her gait was unsteady. There were more people—I counted more than ten—and all of them seemed to be unsure of themselves. Joshua let them all in.

He said to me, "Sir, this is my mother. I told her to come. These people are our neighbors. They came here to be safe."

I nodded. His words were in my head: They came here to be safe. Joshua's mother was now sobbing, quietly, but because of the night it seemed she was crying loudly. I looked at the others, the neighbors; there were three full families, some young men and two young ladies.

One of the young men spoke, "We live very close to one of the polling booths. So they started with us. I don't know how many they have killed."

"There's space here for everyone," I said.

Joshua's mother sobbed louder; his brother held her. "Ma, take it easy, take it easy now." No one else cried.

I led them to the rectory. Joshua and the young men stayed behind as though they expected something. While we walked I envisaged the things that I would move to make space for them. A low table separated the long settees. If I took away the table there would be space for more chairs; there was a stack of plastic chairs inside my room; I would have to bring them out. We all walked in silence to the residence, only the sound of our footsteps could be heard. Intermittently there were sighs. Otherwise the night was quiet.

I had left the door to the house open and I could hear water from the bathroom tap dripping into the sink. I lit a candle; everyone found a place to stand in the living room. I said, "You're safe here. They will not come here. They will not come here." They only nodded at my repetition; I knew they did not believe me. That was when Joshua's mother said, "I told him politics was madness. I told him," and started sobbing again. Then she added, with a sudden rise in her voice, "Why did they kill him?" No one said anything to her.

I turned on the radio, thinking it would ease the tension. Her sobbing and the radio almost blended perfectly, but when they began to announce the election results again, repeating the figures, I switched it off. It didn't stop Joshua's mother from crying. Soon someone joined her, then another, until almost everyone was wailing. I left them and went to the bathroom to wash my face.

When I could no longer hear them weeping, hoping they were spent, I turned off the tap in the bathroom and returned to the living room. I had to squeeze myself to stand in a position where they could all see me. I said, "I cannot guarantee that they won't come here. So let me show you a safer place. If anything happens just go up there."

My words were met with silent disinterest. Then Joshua's mother said, "Now that he is dead, let me see which party he will join. Let me see, let me see." She did not sob anew, but her words made many of the people sigh noisily.

I beckoned to one of the young men, "Come with me."

I took him and showed him the safer place, the tiny upstairs built into the roof of the rectory, which I had unlocked only twice since taking residence there. It was a dark place, not more than ten feet wide. I knew if there was any option, that was it. But then I remembered reading about Rwanda, how during the genocide the assailants shot into the ceiling, knowing people were hiding up there. It isn't possible, I assured myself. Just before the back door, there was a staircase leading up to the attic. I can't tell why it was built—perhaps it was the work of some adventurous architect some forty years ago, or maybe it was built at the specific request of one of the earlier priests, the British ones possibly. Living there I sometimes felt I was part of an archaeological narrative.

We returned to the sitting room. Some of the people were asleep, some rested their heads on their palms, and others simply sat straight up and cast their eyes down. I wanted to retire to my room, but considered that it would be rude leaving them that way. I knew it was a dangerous thing I was doing; I knew the consequences. But all that was apparent to me at the time was the fact of what I was doing, bringing all those people to the rectory and showing them the attic.

As soon as I returned, Joshua's brother said, "I am going back there." He was slender, unlike Joshua. He did not look like someone who could fight or who sought action.

Even though there was no power supply and the candle did not properly illuminate the living room, I could see Joshua's mother jerk and sit upright when she heard her son's voice. She would have given anything to have misheard. "John? What did you say?"

"I am going back there."

"Why?"

"Please, John," she sobbed.

My inclination was to tell her not to beg him. She should let him go and die. But it seemed necessary to say something else, considering how much she must have suffered already. "John, what are you going there to do?" I asked.

"I know these people, Reverend. I went to school with Dansaki. I know them. And they just come and start killing us. I can do something, I can do something back."

"What, John, what?" his mother intoned; there was no difference between her sob and her voice. Some of those who had been sleeping stirred. Some woke. Those who rested their heads on their palms sat up. Those who were sitting straight reclined.

"I can do something," was John's reply.

He stood up. His mother stood up. This time her voice was commanding, like she would have spoken if John had been six and wanted to put his thumb in the fire.

"John, don't go back there!"

He said, "Ma, I can do something," and walked out. She did not, could not, stop him. No one did.

And no one joined her when she began weeping. I checked the time. It was about 9:00 p.m.

Then I went into the bathroom to wash my face, thinking that when I returned I would take the radio into my room and listen to it there.

We met

In the weeks that led to that night, I was a regular visitor to Gaskiya, a canteen where I could watch football and listen to local gossip. I would sip a drink quietly and talk to no one, just listen and watch. Some who knew me as the priest of the nearby Anglican Church said a passing hello. Most people did not. But Isah, the man who owned Gaskiya, knew me. One evening he sat down beside me.

"Isah."

"Pastor. How now?"

"Fine. You?"

"Small small."

I gulped the rest of my Fanta and looked at Isah more intently, saying nothing.

"I'm a Muslim, you know?"

"Of course."

"But I want my boy to come to your church school."

My church ran a primary school; I directly supervised its affairs.

I took some time before I asked, "Why?"

"Exposure, that's all."

"Exposure?"

"Yes. I'm an open-minded person."

I asked, "Have you told your people?"

"Which people?"

"Other Muslims."

"Why? I'm not accountable to anyone."

"They could see it differently, you know."

Isah paused and bowed his head. When he looked up he said, "You've not given me a response. Can you register him or not? Can he come to your school?"

"That is not a problem at all. No problem."

"Are you sure?"

I hesitated because I feared Isah would notice the inconsistency in my voice. "Sure. He can come."

Isah took my hand, "Thank you. Thank you, Pastor."

But all the while I was uncertain, feeling I was making a terrible mistake.

The mistake was confirmed when I was invited by the Transition Committee to an inter-faith clerical meeting. In a letter addressed to me I was labeled a "respected religious leader," a compliment that I knew was simply copied and pasted into all the invitation letters. I decided to go for the same reason I would have objected—there was no point going, and no point staying, and then I considered that it might be beneficial, after all.

When the day came I wore a simple suit with a black tie, no priestly collar; I did not carry a Bible, just my journal, in which I usually recorded appointments and sundry irrelevancies.

The chairman of the Transition Committee waited until it was time for a break before he introduced me to the group of clerics sitting around a table. There was no applause, only the nodding of heads and then a man sitting by his side shook my hand. He was a pastor too, but his suit smelled damp. I smiled to the others, counting while I smiled. There were ten men in all, only two of whom wore turbans.

When we resumed—I spent the break doodling in my journal—the chairman talked about how religious leaders were pivotal to ensuring that the people came out to vote, for everyone, he said, has a religion here. He added that religious leaders were the custodians of peace.

"That is all I have to say. Any questions or comments?"

"I have a comment to make," one of the men wearing a turban said.

"Go on, sir," was the chairman's response.

I saw that his black face held dull eyes, as though he had seen too much and had become tired of seeing.

"Religion and politics are two different things."

"I don't understand you, sir," the chairman said.

"That is all I wanted to say." I thought I saw the man's eye gain some sharpness, but then lose it immediately. When the man did not say anything further, the chairman went on to repeat his speech on the role of religious leaders.

Then it was time to go, and the chairman asked, "Reverend, do you have anything to say?" and I said, "No. No, sir."

While everyone else exchanged pleasantries, I looked at a painting on the wall. The other pastor joined me and said, "It's beautiful, isn't it?"

"Yes," I turned to him, "it is an impasto."

"Oh."

Another voice behind us said, "It is not an impasto. Impasto is a technique." I turned. It was the man who had spoken about religion and politics. He continued, "When paint is applied thickly, so that brush marks are evident, that's when it is an impasto." He concluded and smiled; this time I was sure about his face and his dull eyes.

I smiled to the other man, "I am sorry for misleading you." All three of us laughed.

"Reverend, can I have a word with you?"

"Of course."

The man wearing the turban took me aside and said, gripping my hands, "I am the chief imam of the Central Mosque."

"Nice meeting you. *Assalamu alaikum.*"

He laughed heartily, "*Wa alaikum assalaam.*" There was a little pause and then he said, "You must be very careful, Reverend. People are not happy that you accepted Isah's son to your church school. He is a Muslim. There are things we do not joke with, things that are very sensitive. That is why we might go the extra mile to protect our religion, our practice and beliefs. So, you must be careful."

I wanted to ask, "So, what do you want me to do?" but the chairman called out to us to join in the group photograph, and I didn't have the temerity to ask him that anyway. The imam looked at me, but when I met his gaze, he took his eyes away, his dull-looking eyes.

After the group photograph the imam told the photographer, "Both of us."

It ended like that, a photograph with the imam — it was the only significant thing that happened at the meeting.

Two days later, a gap-toothed man came to see me. He smiled a lot, as if he wanted to show off the space between his teeth. The smile seemed fixed, and I considered it fake.

"I'm contesting for the chairmanship of the local government."

"That's fine."

"Yes. I want you to help me."

I smiled, saying, "You know I am not a politician."

The man's fixed smile reinvented itself: this time broader, showing yellow patches on the rest of his teeth. "Of course, I know. But you don't have to be a politician to help me."

"How do I help you, then?"

"Tell your church people. Announce to them that I am capable."

"Oh." I said, smiling.

"I have a copy of my manifesto here. I have very good intentions. I have the interest of the people."

"I will do my best."

"Please. I am not an Hausa man and I heard they want to hijack this election."

"Why are you worried about that?"

"Jos has been sitting on gunpowder for a long time. These crazy Hausa people are waiting for any slight opportunity."

"Oh. I honestly don't care about your Hausa hate speech." After a while the man said, "Just help me. Talk to your church people."

"Okay."

The man was about to leave when I said, "You have not told me your name."

"I'm sorry. Daniel Tyokighir."

"Okay, Mr. Tyokighir. I'll do my best."

He left without another word, just a handshake. He even forgot to leave his manifesto. After he left, I cleared my table for the day and went to the rectory to sleep. I determined not to talk about the elections in the church; I was not going to get involved. I had come to Jos to escape. The meeting with Mr. Tyokighir would've had no significance if I hadn't met with Olisa, who attended my church. He was Igbo, and like many Igbos in Jos he was a businessman—a spare parts dealer.

He came to me and asked me to pray for his new shop.

I said to him, "Why do you want me to pray for your shop?"

"Honestly, Reverend, I am afraid."

Then I remembered Mr. Tyokighir, his manifesto, the fact that he was not Hausa. "What are you afraid of?" I asked him.

"Anything can happen. This is not our land. Our home is far away."

"This is not our land?"

"Yes. It's simply because we wanted to eat. Simple."

I wanted to say no, I was not there to eat, simply. But I didn't trust he would understand, seeing my reasons for coming to Jos were even unclear to me.

"You want me to pray for your shop?"

"Yes."

"Let's go."

There were things I had to do—the following day was Sunday. But I knew that, for my own sake, I had to attend to Olisa promptly. The fear was beginning to get to me, the fear of things that could happen now that the elections were approaching. If I prayed maybe I would be relieved of the fear that hung on my heart like a millstone.

Before I left my office—a small room behind the vestry—I said, "You are not going to make me scared." He looked at me for a considerably long time, sitting while I was already standing, and said, "I must have some sense, Reverend. I am not a coward. I must take precautions."

And because his answer was infused with an intelligence I had not imagined he possessed, I said, without thinking, "So this prayer you want is a precaution?"

"Yes. Our prayers can do what we cannot do. I have friends who have gotten charms for their shops and their houses. But I don't believe in charms. I believe in Jesus."

"So this prayer can keep any evil from your shop?"

"Yes, Reverend, I'm surprised you are asking me."

I shook my head, smiled, and said, "Let's go."

I believe that was the moment I began to doubt the impossibility of tragedy. Thinking about an inevitable downfall was akin to losing my faith, for I was taught to trust in and preach about God's saving grace, his ability to reach to humankind in the farthest depths, his protection in the Valley of Shadows. But I was quickly losing grip of this conviction. As usual, when I needed to contemplate my beliefs for the sake of clarity, I sought a place outside the church compound. Gaskiya was my best bet. There I met Olisa again. It was a week after I had prayed for his new shop. It was also the day before the elections.

He told me he had come for a drink, to clear his head. I told him I was there to clear my head too. He smiled. It was when he sat facing me that I realized that Gaskiya had lost its congested feel, the crowd that was always there. There were empty tables and few customers. Isah came to us. Earlier I had waved him off, but now Olisa was here.

"What do you want?" he asked, looking at Olisa.

"A beer for me," Olisa said.

"Reverend?"

"A beer for me too."

"Reverend?" Olisa asked, with surprise.

"The last time I drank beer was seven years ago. I was terribly scared that night."

"Are you scared today?"

I laughed. Isah brought the beers.

He pressed, "Are you scared, Reverend?"

"Of what? Of what, Olisa?"

Olisa bowed his head; he took a sip from his beer, and then looked up, not at me. "That's why you want to clear your head? You're scared." Now he looked at me.

"What has *you* afraid?" I asked him.

"I don't know."

"Your business?"

"I don't know."

"Your family?"

"I don't know."

"Survival?"

"I said I don't know, Reverend."

I sipped my beer and then spat it out. It was too bitter. My spittle formed a pool on the table. I was embarrassed, but Olisa laughed, "Seven years is a long time."

"Yes," I said, but took another swig.

Olisa suddenly asked, "Tell me the truth. Are you scared?"

"Why should I be scared? Eh?"

"The rumors are stronger. They say they have brought in mercenaries from Kano and Borno, even Chad. They say the election will definitely end in violence."

"I am not scared, Olisa."

"Oh God," he said, rubbing his face. It seemed as if he wanted to cry. For some time we sat in silence, drinking our beers and staring mindlessly at the football match on TV.

After a while I stood up and walked away from the table; Olisa followed. When we got outside, I noticed posters opposite the road, on the door of a cyber café, which read, "Polling Center." We did not look at each other.

Olisa had come in a car. He asked me to get in, asked if I was going to the church. We drove in silence, and when we got to the church, we said nothing to each other. But I noticed that Olisa hesitated before he drove away.

She came

I couldn't tell why she came. I was, in truth, distracted by her beauty. At that time I was not worried about remaining a bachelor. While I recurrently had wet dreams and occasionally made passes at beautiful women among my laity, there was no urge. I just had a fleeting feeling of sexuality, the kind that was reluctantly ambitious. None of this changed when she came into my office. Her beauty took hold of me in the way it should have, and I found myself staring at her lips, and once or twice at her breasts.

She must have guessed that I was carried away, so she sat before I asked her to.

"My name is Taibat," she said, offering an opening into the conversation.

"I am Muna. Munachimso."

"You are Igbo, then?"

I nodded. I saw the mischief in her smile. But it was temporary mischievousness; her face seemed equally burdened by a lingering concern.

"I will just say what I came here to say."

"Okay."

She hesitated. I waited for her to speak. She fondled the handle of her handbag. She scratched her face. I sat up, placed my elbows on my desk, held my head with my hands.

"You know this is difficult for me. I am not a garrulous person." I nodded, hoping I had successfully disguised my eagerness and confusion. "I am just telling you this because I don't want you to die a stupid death." She said this and looked at me, met my eyes. She blinked on and on but she still looked at me. And it was impossible for me to forget that exchange afterward: her eyelids blinking on and on, my eyes steady, the word "death" circling my head like a noose.

"I don't understand you."

"You can't understand."

I said, spitefully, "I can't understand? My death is imminent and I can't understand?"

"I am here to tell you all that I know."

"How can I know you are telling me all that you know?"

"You must trust me."

"That's a big word. Trust."

She said nothing. I removed my elbows from the desk, folded my arms. "They are planning an attack and you're a target. This church and you."

I wanted to say it was nonsense. "Who are these people planning an attack?"

"That's none of your business." She stood up. I stood up too. She said, "Just leave here. Take your things and leave."

On other days I would have followed my visitors to the door. But I figured that if I did so it would be useless, she would not appreciate it. I did not intend to think about dying, my possible death, or her unconfirmed information.

She came again, this time to the rectory. It was one of those evenings when, tired of listening to the radio, I sat on a bench outside and read a book. My library at that time was a modest collection of books on theology, thriller novels by Dean Koontz, a dozen Mills & Boon publications, a dozen Pacesetters, and a handful of motivational books. The evening she came I was reading one of the Mills & Boon romance novels. All she said when she came close was, "I came to warn you again."

I asked her, "You want something to drink? Anything?" By this time I was standing, nervous at her presence, thinking that I could have an affair with her, a lady I only knew by first name.

She sat on the bench. "Just water."

I went into the rectory and returned with a glass and a bottle of water. She took the bottle from me and poured herself a glass. When she was through with drinking she capped the bottle and set it beside her. I was standing, and I noticed her dress for the first time. It was patterned with flowers I couldn't identify, sleeveless, and had a collar. She wore a scarf around her head, tied so neatly that her ears didn't show.

"You're looking at me," she said.

"You are beautiful," I replied.

She chuckled and looked to the distance. I saw that even her laugh was tempered with the same lingering concern she had the first time we met.

"It's surprising you say that. A priest."

"A priest is blind to beauty?"

"Expectedly."

I laughed and she did too. I came and sat beside her on the bench, so that the half-empty bottle and the glass formed a boundary between us.

"Did you think about what I said?"

"What?"

She shook her head, her face creased into a frown, as though she was annoyed at my insensitivity. But when she spoke next her voice contained more concern than anger. "I told you to leave here."

"I did not give much thought to it, honestly."

"It is good I came, then."

"Yes," I said, thinking it was good she came because I was sitting beside her.

"I am serious about what I said. I am taking a risk to tell you what I heard."

It was this second meeting with Taibat, which followed my first meeting with Olisa that inscribed the feeling of an inevitable tragedy in me. Having lived a quiet life since I had come to Jos, I found it appalling, even irreverent, that I would be targeted for death. It made no sense.

"How did you hear what you heard?"

I knew she understood the implication of that question—I needed to trust her. I wouldn't leave Jos if I didn't trust her.

"My father is the head of all the Yoruba Muslims here. He told me what he overheard. He told me just so I could know how bad things were getting."

I asked her, "What did he tell you?"

"I have told you what he told me."

"And what is that?"

She raised her hands to explain a point, but dropped the thought. She said nothing and stood up. "Just think about what I've said."

I didn't want to argue. "I will walk with you to the gate," I said.

She shook her head. "You should worry."

While Taibat walked alone to the gate I thought of how much effort she must have put into her scarf, tying it so that her ears did not show.

She came a final time, on the eve of the election. It was the same day Olisa met me in Gaskiya. This time, she came after nightfall; this time she knocked on my door and I opened and saw it was her. I was neither surprised nor excited—being nervous only helped to create a bland sense of wonder. Although I knew our friendship was going to take a different turn that night, I knew that if I wasn't careful things would get out of hand and I would be blamed.

"You won't let me in?" she asked, smiling. The light was poor. The electric bulb hanging overhead provided little light. In those days the supply ranged between nothing and low voltage. So, at certain times, the only reasonable thing to do was put off the lights and ceiling fans, open the windows, and leave the radio on.

"I'm sorry," I said, moving from the doorway.

"I'm sorry, coming to your house at this time," she said when she was inside. I was ashamed of the darkness but she sat on the loveseat. I sat next to her, keeping a reasonable distance between us, thinking of what to say. In five years of living alone, this was the first time that a lady was in my house after nightfall.

"You shouldn't be sorry. You are my friend."

She laughed when I said this, laughter that was depthless.

"You want anything?" I asked. I felt foolish. I realized it sounded as though I was asking why she came when I was actually asking if she wanted something to drink or eat. There was yam porridge in the kitchen, a few drinks in the refrigerator, a loaf of bread, and a tin of sardines. Yet I had asked a question with many possible meanings and unintended consequences.

She told me why she had come. Her home was filled with visitors who had come to celebrate her father's return from Mecca, a trip that he took two months before. They were relatives and well-wishers who had only come to celebrate, eat, and ask for transportation fare for their return trip. She said that no visitors had slept over when her mother had died. They had just come and left, crying inside the house, laughing outside. Now they filled the house and made it difficult for her to breathe.

I asked her, "Your mother died?"

"Yes, last year."

"Of what?"

"I think it was cancer. I don't know. She just died."

I waited a while. I said, "My mother died too." I expected her to ask me "of what" but she didn't. It was a question I wouldn't have answered anyway. The fact of my mother's death hung like an unsaid word over our heads. I continued to allow the significant physical distance between us. I noticed her hair was not covered in a scarf, just free and flowing. I retained the thought—free and flowing.

In that period when there was silence, her face was unmoving. In the low light I saw she was crying. I covered the significant distance between us, moved close to her, my right arm over her shoulder, my left palm wiped her eyes. "You shouldn't cry," I said. She cried even more, steadily. I left my arm over her shoulder, but I dropped my left hand, so that her tears flowed freely. The next moment, perhaps after a minute, she was through with crying. I considered taking my arm away when she wiped her eyes, but she didn't show the slightest opposition.

"I am afraid. It's tomorrow," she said.

"The elections?"

"You're just unbelievably foolish." I heard the anger in her voice. But her assault was weak, and I saw that when she looked at me after she said "foolish" her eyes were not colored with menace. Maybe she was sorry for sounding angry.

"That's a cruel thing for you to say," I replied.

"I'm sorry. It's just because, just because you're still here."

"This place is my life. If I leave here I am dead inside, I tell you. It's like choosing between dying and dying." When I said this I remembered what I had read once, maybe Hemingway. That it was possible to have courage without imagination.

I realized she was the kind of person who left questions unasked. I hoped she'd ask me to tell her what had happened before I came to Jos. She moved her neck so I could take my arm off her shoulder. I did. But she drew closer to me, put her head on my chest. The aroma of her hair cream reminded me of the ocean.

"I am sorry for saying you're foolish."

"I wasn't offended."

"Can I stay here for the night? I could sleep here."

"It's not a problem." I thought again of unintended consequences, like sex, like Joshua confronting me afterward, saying he'd heard some noise.

"I was bored, and I only thought of your place. I don't have many friends."

"Why not many friends?"

"I schooled outside here. Ilorin."

"I have never been to Ilorin."

"That's a shame. It's kind of a gateway town. The people there are almost like the people in the North. I think Islam got there before any other Yoruba town. My grandfather built a mosque there." The head on my chest and the hair that smelled like the ocean were all I could think about. Yet she kept talking. "I once considered being a Christian. But I didn't see the point. And then I was scared of my family. My father is a fanatic Yoruba Muslim. I love him so much, and I can't lose his love."

The only response I gave was, "Hmm." Again, she did not press for details, did not ask what my thoughts on the subject were. I should have stood up for Christianity, convinced her that it was the only way to God, that Prophet Mohammed was a demonic construct, as some believed, imagined only to avert gazes from the one true savior, Jesus Christ.

Yet the only clear thought in my head was that her free and flowing hair was spread over my chest.

"I want to sleep now," she said and stood. I stood too, and faced her. She looked at me and understood my intentions. When I kissed her she remained still. I brought my face close to hers again but she turned her cheek.

"I came here to talk, just talk," she said.

"I am sorry."

"I'll just go. We can't do this."

I wanted to ask her why, but I said, "No, you shouldn't go. I'm being stupid."

"It's been a long time?"

"What?"

"Sex."

"Yes," I replied uncomfortably. "Yes."

She said, "I've never..." but did not complete her sentence. It was an awkward moment. I knew it was a fleeting passion on my part. I knew nothing could work in the long term, seeing as I was a priest and she was the daughter of a Yoruba Muslim. We stood facing each other. I couldn't tell what she was thinking while she looked at me with pity. But the kind of pity she showed was empathetic: When she pitied me she pitied herself too. She sat back down on the loveseat.

"I'll just sleep here."

"No, no. You'll stay in the room. I'll sleep here. I'll go now and make the bed."

She nodded. Before I entered my room I washed my face in the bathroom. Because the light was poor I caught my hazy reflection in the mirror. There was no recognizable expression, just my face. I felt increasingly sinful while I made the bed for Taibat.

She woke me up and told me she had had a bad dream. "I just saw you running." I said nothing. And she held my hands. It was then I saw that she was sitting on the floor, her face close to mine as I lay on the couch. She must have been sitting there for a long while.

"I just saw you running," she said again. There was no hint of fear in her voice.

"Are you afraid?" I asked, knowing my assumption could be wrong.

"I don't know what I feel. I am just expectant."

"That's good."

"Yes, good."

Her hand was caressing my head. The low light was still on and I could see her smile. I wondered what time it was. I glanced at the clock but couldn't quite tell. "You know what time it is?" I asked. Her hand was still on my head. She caressed my face tenderly.

"No. But we couldn't have slept long."

"Okay."

Her hand was still on my head when she said, "Let's sing."

"A song?"

"Of course a song."

"What song?"

"You sing the song that comes to your head first and I'll do the same."

There was no song in my head and I told her.

"I will sing the song in my head first, and then you," she said. She sang:

La la la la la la la la
La la la la la la la la
La la la la la la
La la la la la la
La la la la la la
La la la la

"Is that all the song in your head?" I asked.

"Yes," she said, chuckling.

"You'll sing it again after I sing mine?"

"Just sing yours."

I sang mine:

It's a new dawn,
It's a new day
It's a new life
For me
And I'm feeling good.

"There's too much meaning in that one. It spoils the fun," she said.

"I like the part that says 'I'm feeling good.'"

She rubbed my head and said, "I feel good too." Then she traced my eyelashes with one of her fingers. She didn't remember to sing her song again, but I remembered her song.

I can't tell when I slept again, but I guess her hand remained on my head until I fell asleep. When I awoke she was gone. I thought of her hair then, and the smell of the ocean.

His prophecy

I left the people in my living room and walked to the church. I checked the clock before I left: 1:30 a.m. I pushed the door, which was unlocked, and went inside. I sat in one of the back pews. I did not want to think about Taibat, I just wanted to remember her song. Yet I did not remember how she had sequenced the *la la*, or how many times she had sung it. So I thought instead of where she could be at that time, if her family was affected. If, as I gathered, it was an ethno-religious affair, I wondered if her father would be spared, given he was Yoruba. But I freed myself of such

88

thoughts. I simply stared into the darkness, sitting in a pew I had never previously sat in.

It was because of the darkness in the church that the light from behind was blinding. I turned, having dozed off, shielding my eyes from the bright light, and saw that a man was approaching. With him there were four smaller persons, children maybe. The man had a huge rechargeable battery-powered lamp. I stood from the pew, my head pounding.

As they came closer I recognized the man.

"Olisa!" I called.

"Reverend," he responded. The four children sat on one of the pews, huddled together. On a normal day they would have sat here for Sunday school, for an exciting lesson about Jesus or Judas.

"Reverend, they have started the attacks."

"I have heard."

"You see what I told you? You see that I was not lying."

I shook my head, wanting to smile. He sounded euphoric at the fulfillment of his prophecy.

"Let us go to my house."

"No, Reverend. We will stay here."

"It is not safe here. I have an attic. It's safer there. There are people there."

"Where is safe, Reverend? I thought it was safe to vote for the Hausa man. But it does not make any difference now, no difference that I voted for him. This is where I want to stay. In this church. If I die, let me die here." His voice was raised and at the same time low, like a tremolo, a jumbled fluctuation.

I wanted to say, "Don't be foolhardy, think about your children, look at the four of them." But I didn't. I wanted to take his children out of the church, but I knew that the decision wasn't mine to make. When I was outside Olisa said, "Reverend," with that same wavering voice. He said nothing more. It was then that I remembered the sequence of Taibat's song, the exact way she sang it. And I sang it under my breath while I walked back to the rectory.

Seven years is a long time

After Taibat's first visit, that day at my office when she warned me to leave, I wrote a letter to my brother. It would be a lie to say I didn't think of dying; maybe I thought of it in a different way, death as the inability to reach my brother and my father. It was the first letter I had hand-written in seven years.

Dear Chuka,

After seven years you must think that I no longer exist, that God has made me pay for my wrongs. Yes, I have paid. I have become a priest of the Anglican Church. You remember Venerable Madu? I went to him and he told me he felt God's call is on my life. Then he wrote a letter to his friend in Bukuru, that theological school, and his friend, the registrar, admitted me.

How is Papa? This is a very short letter; it took me a lot of courage to write it. I hope it gets to you. Tell Papa I am alive, and well. I have missed you all, I didn't believe I would. Can you reply? My email address is munachimsojos@yahoo.com. Please reply. If you can please give me Papa's number so I can speak to him.

Muna

After I called Joshua and gave him the letter to mail, I closed my eyes. It was hard to shut out my mother's face. She was there in my head, right there, that moment when I pushed her away from me and she fell and landed on her back. Right there when she fell and landed on the welder's unused metal rod, the sharp one fixed to the ground. The sharp one that stuck out half-buried in the ground after many months of rusting away unused.

My mother held my shirt before I pushed her. She was calling me a useless boy, good for nothing, a shame-trotter, a jobless boy, a male prostitute. This was not the first time, not the second. I was living with my parents in Enugu, two years after I had finished university. I pushed my mother when I was angry at her voice, at the embarrassment she was causing me, right there in the street where she'd met me on her way to the market. Right there in front of the welder's shop, close to our house. Right there where there was unused metal partially buried in the ground.

During my mother's burial my father did not look at me, not even a glance. My only brother, who was younger, spoke in monosyllables and he avoided my eye when he uttered even those meager words.

This was the tragedy that made me leave, that made me say nothing to anyone about where I was going. I went to Venerable Madu, because the only rational thing I thought to do was visit my priest and tell him I had pushed my mother to her death. I had pushed her to the metal that made her bleed and lose so much blood. I told him it was a lie what everyone said—that she fell accidentally—a lie told by my father and brother. And that the welder, who should have told the truth, repeated this lie when he was asked. That was when Venerable Madu prayed with me and said he felt God's call on my life, a call I didn't hear or feel.

My brother's reply came via email. His message was longer than mine. I checked my email twice a week at a cyber café close to Gaskiya, the place that would be used as a polling booth.

My Dear Brother,

When I got your letter I did not know what to think. You might expect that I did not miss you, that your going was a good riddance to bad rubbish. I expected that too. But six months later, I wanted you back; it did not matter if you had killed Mama or not. I have so much to write in this letter, so bear with me if it is too long. I am not writing on one single sheet like you did; thank God for email. You don't know how mad I was when I received your letter. I ran around the house shouting, dancing, screaming. Seven years is not seven days.

When I told Papa that you wrote to me, he called your name and asked if I was sure, but did not say anything more. He has gotten over the shock of Mama's death. But that day, when he heard you wrote to me he did not come out to eat dinner, but stayed inside his room and played loud music. He still loves listening to Elton John, Michael Bolton, and Stevie Wonder, sometimes Elvis Presley. I think it was music that healed him early because even when I hear the songs I do not feel angry again, I just think about good things.

You said you have become a priest. A priest! When I think about all the things you did, especially your notoriety with women, I cannot reconcile my brother with being a priest. But it is a good thing. They say God can change anybody. The morning after I got your letter I told Papa you were now a priest in Jos. He said, "Are you sure?" I said "Yes." Then he said, "There's nothing impossible." He said it twice. I left home soon after I finished university and moved to Lagos. But I am not in Lagos anymore. I had a good career working as a copywriter, but I do not regret leaving it behind. I came to work for Papa, to take control of his business. One day Papa called me to come home, he did not say why. When I got home he was sleeping in the front yard on that long grandfather chair, and I was surprised that he was there at 11:00 p.m. I woke him up. He did not say welcome, he just said, "Chu, I have cancer."

The next day he told me I had to take over his business, to control it. "If your brother was here he would have been the one, as the first born," he told me that after I told him that you wrote me. He smiled and I smiled too. Then he told me not to tell you that when I replied your letter. When I asked why, he said nothing but went inside and played a Kenny Rogers song and I can remember that the volume was high and it made me think of nothing, just the voice of Kenny Rogers filling the house.

There is a feeling of death everywhere in the house. I am always thinking that he can die at any time, and I am afraid. If Mama were here maybe it would have been different. If you were here maybe it would be different too.

But I am alone.

Papa has started talking about marriage for me. He said you must be married now, that your head must have settled. And he keeps inferring that he might not be here longer. He annoys me when he says this, because he says it with so much sarcasm and confidence, and even expectation. I am also annoyed because at the end it seems I am the only one afraid. Tell me, are you married now? You know I cannot get married if you are not married. A younger brother should not get married before his elder brother. Yet I can say I have found the woman I want to marry. Bridget. She laughs all the time. That is what I like about her. Laughter is good for this life. Father says he likes her too, though I am not sure if it is the marriage he accepts or Bridget: those are two different things.

Let me end by asking what Papa said I should ask: when are you coming to see us? We want to see you again. They say the old things have passed away, all things are new. We want to see you again.

When you reply tell me when you are coming. I may fix my wedding after that.

Please reply.

Chu

All I did was copy his email, address chuka4real4u@yahoo.com, into my journal. It was the day before I met with Olisa in Gaskiya, the day before the elections. I knew that soon I would think of composing a reply, now that my father and my brother wanted to see me again.

They came

When I heard the shouts around 5:30 a.m. of someone who sounded like Joshua, I walked out of my bedroom and into the sitting room. The people hiding out in the living room must have heard the shouts too, because they were all standing when I walked in. I was surprised that Joshua's mother was not crying. I signaled to the young man who knew the about the attic. "Let's go," I said. Someone among the people asked, "Is it them?" Everyone must have heard the question, but no one answered.

I led them to the attic, staying behind while they climbed up. Not one of them complained about the tiny space, about how they were being crammed in. When all of them were hidden, I stared at the staircase, thinking that if I was a sincere priest I would've prayed with them, prayed the twenty-third Psalm, and said grace.

I went to the living room and sat. I thought of escape, but I feared that if I climbed into the attic they would search there, find me and the others. Then I remembered Olisa and his children, because there were new shouts. Yet it was becoming difficult to think, because all things at that moment were thinkable, all possibilities became relevant. So I decided to think of nothing, trying again in vain to remember Taibat's song.

Then they came; faces appeared in my living room. I stood up before they asked me to. I looked around the living room, and realized I was alone.

II

There are times when I am dying but I feel like I'm being born again. There are other times when I believe that the world is not spherical, but a straight line. We keep moving, never looking back. I like to think that God found me, that he saw me as one who was in need of something that couldn't be defined, and he gave me my life back. It didn't matter that my life didn't mean much; there were those who didn't survive the post-election crisis in Jos. I have not given much thought to essence, or to why I survived.

There are times when I climb the altar and look at everyone sitting and staring up at me. Then I feel that my life is yet to begin. But I am thirty-six, closer to forty than not.

The only thing I remember is being carried up, with the noise having ceased. I was told the police came to the church, or what was left of it, and the men who had been carrying machetes and calling Allah disappeared. I was told other things, fables perhaps: that the men suddenly took to their heels and a schizophrenic passerby helped me up, took me to a nearby clinic. But nothing seemed more questionable than the arrival of the police or the passing of a brave schizophrenic. I have lived with that question, and sometimes I have tried to forget it.

I am talking with the Bishop of the Jos Diocese and he is saying sorry to me, saying these things are bad for the church, for the name of God. I expect him to speak of persecution, but he does not. Instead he speaks of how privileged I am to be alive, how miraculous, and how he is afraid that peace is not coming, that things will get worse. Then he says to me that he wants me to leave Jos, to get some fresh air. I tell him I do not know what I want and he nods, understandingly. He says he wants me to go to the Southwest, he has friends there—it was where he worked before being made Bishop of this Diocese. He wants me to apply for the position of Assistant Chaplain of the Interdenominational Chapel in the old University of Ife, now named after Chief Obafemi Awolowo, a rechristening he doesn't endorse.

So I come to the Southwest without feeling. It is just like the absence of feeling that accompanies breathing. Before I take up the position in the interdenominational chapel, I go home. Upon seeing my father and my brother, I start to cry. They start

95

to cry too, even before we hug each other. I walk with a limp now; it is the scar of survival. So when anyone who knew me before Jos sees me, they know something is different. I say to my father and brother that I am very sorry—I kneel. My father helps me up, saying forgiveness is the way to renewal. He speaks about forgiveness in a way that makes me unsure of myself. I do not know whether I have forgiven the men who gave me a limp, who attacked my church, who killed Olisa and his children, and Joshua.

Every time I stand facing the congregation, I can't tell if I'm feeling. I say the words as they exist in my head, with perfunctory precision, arithmetic compulsion. Whether leading a prayer or reciting the creed or preparing for communion, I make no effort.

But things change.

The Chaplain calls me to his office and says he wants all the units in the chapel to hold retreats—a time off when they can evaluate their operational pattern, seek change, and recommit themselves to God's work. I nod in agreement. I remember thinking of having looked at myself in the mirror that morning and having seen a distanced man. It was as though I was the infamous shadow that existed between dreams and reality. I nod to the Chaplain without asking any questions of logistics or practicality.

"So what do you say?"

"It's okay."

"Okay. Good. Are you fine?"

"Yes, Sir. I am fine."

He asks me if I am fine each time we meet. I always answer the same way. I give him no room to assume anything, as I am living and acting without thinking, without assumptions.

He says, "I am thinking we should see the leaders personally, you know, all the heads of the units. To make them understand why we need to do this."

"That's okay."

"Yes. So I'm thinking you should see the Choirmaster."

"Of course."

"Good."

"When are we looking at for the retreats?"

"I think two weeks is perfect."

"Right."

It is always like this. He says he is thinking about something, implying that his thoughts are suggestive, inconclusive. But each time I answer him in a way that shows that I am not ready to think of anything, that we can follow his plan. He has not complained, but I know it won't be long before he does; I have been waiting for someone to challenge my competence, to suggest that I am aloof to the chapel's progress, even to the service of God. So far, that has not happened.

I spend an enormous amount of time talking with my brother on the phone. He is married now. We talk about our father's imminent death each time; how it is miraculous that he is not already dead. Miraculous—a word we know is dubious. Each time we talk Chuka tells me that I am different. He says it as though he knows my Jos life. If he knew my Jos life, he would be right to guess that I have undergone various changes. I am not the man I was when I left home after my mother's burial. I am not the man I was when I lived in Jos. And I've become a different person since I left Jos. It is the only thing I am certain about; that I am different. Yet, I cannot locate the parameters of that difference.

"You should get married."

"Why?"

"Marriage changes a person. Look at me."

"There are no women here."

"That's funny and stupid."

"That's good then. I can still crack jokes."

"You are not being fair to yourself. This is not who you are. Or what you should be doing to yourself."

"You're insulting me."

It's normal for our conversations to end unceremoniously. Toward the end of our talks I usually tell him that he is insulting me, I always end the call. I know I will call him the next day and tell him again that he was insulting me, or find an excuse to end the call abruptly. He never complains about this. If anything he seems to conform to a pattern: saying things that anger me and making me hang up. Then I end up calling him again the following day.

I do not talk with my father much. Mostly I send text messages. I have never been comfortable speaking with him, and I cannot, for instance, remember the contours on his face, because I have scarcely examined his face closely. It seems amazing when I say I have scarcely examined my father's face. But the fact is that I cannot trace his visage in my mind. Yet, I am familiar with his voice, for my mind often speaks to me with his voice.

While I prepare to go to the Choirmaster's house, I listen to a TED Talk on my laptop. A professor of war economics is speaking on an economic model that will bring an end to the war in Afghanistan. I have become deeply interested in war since I came to Ife. It amazes me that when I wake up on some mornings, I think that I am a wartime hero, a battle-time legend. I am currently reading everything I can find on the wars in Iraq and Afghanistan; each time I ask myself what I would do if I heard that the wars had ended. I find that I am too interested in them, and it might hurt me when they end, because there would be nothing left to feed my imagination, the color that is left in my life.

The Choirmaster's house is in the senior staff quarters. I live outside campus, in Eleyele, so I drive into campus. If the Chapel did not give me an official car, I doubt that I would have bought one. I cannot say what happened to my car in Jos, not that I care. Driving into campus I imagine driving so fast that the car begins to fly. In my mind I fly for the sake of flying, without destination in mind. It is not much different from my actual journey: I am going to the Choirmaster for the sake of going.

His house is L-shaped. There are flowers around it, but it is clear that no one has trimmed them in a long while. It is also clear his house is hardly visited, because it takes some time before his daughter opens the front door. She is unsure of which way to turn the lock, but turns it correctly after two tries. When I enter she says nothing and goes to the back. I take the hint that I should stand until she returns. There are only two photographs in the sitting room and a piano beside one of the settees. The photographs are of the Choirmaster in an academic gown, possibly when he received his M.A. In this photograph he looks plump, well fed, and his smile is assertive. In the second photograph he stands with his wife and their daughters, three in all. They seem to have an agreement not to touch. They stand apart, independent, without sentiment. I also catch a glimpse of a record player. I am not in any way surprised to see it, to find that there is also a 21-inch television and no other appliance.

I hear shuffling feet, and when I look down the hallway I see the Choirmaster walking behind his daughter. She sees me standing but says nothing. It is the Choirmaster who says, "Sit down, Reverend." I smile at him, hoping my mood is imperceptible, as hard to guess as his is. I speak first.

"How are things, Sir?"

"Good. We are coping."

"Thank God."

His daughter comes in with a tray, on which there is a bottle of Coke. She sets it on a stool before me. She leaves and I touch the bottle and find that it is dusty. The Choirmaster sits opposite me. There is a table dividing us that seems as dusty as the bottle of Coke. I decide to take my mind off their hospitality and the ambience.

"The Chaplain asked me to see you."

"Mhmm."

"Yes."

"What for?"

"He wants every service unit in the church to hold a retreat."

"Retreat?"

"Yes."

"What retreat? What for?"

"For evaluation of their work, so far. To meet with new challenges, and see how they can serve God better."

"That's very interesting."

From his face I guess he is in his late-fifties, which means he must have been born in the early 1950s. He would have witnessed Nigeria's independence at an age when he would be sure to remember it. He must have gone to school in a Nigeria that was coming of age; he must have witnessed the time before the oil boom. I preoccupy myself with these contemplations, so that when he speaks I hear him faintly.

"I didn't hear what you said, Sir."

"I have been Choirmaster for twenty five years. We have never done any retreat."

I do not know what to say. I am not prepared for anything of this sort, any dint of opposition. Now that I sense resistance, I can't respond. I am the kind of person who has to prepare for hostility. I tell him what I think, what comes to my head. "I don't understand you, Sir."

"Reverend Muna, I have been Choirmaster all these years and we did not need a retreat. I do not think we need one now. You'll tell that to the Chaplain."

"Okay, then." It is difficult for me to hide my confusion; I stand without opening the Coke. He stands too, adjusting his spectacles, which I believe he must have bought in the Nineties, or even earlier.

"You are not taking your drink?"

"No, Sir. I have to see the Chaplain."

"You have to understand that I'm not used to big changes."

"Yes. I understand."

The next day, while the choir sings, I see that many are not paying attention. There is a collective calm, bordering, I feel, on disenchantment. This is not the first time I have seen such lull. But right now my head feels open, and I realize that it has been closed all along.

When service ends I approach the Choirmaster and tell him that the Chaplain would like to see him. He says he'll be there in a jiffy. I try to avoid his look but our eyes meet and he turns away before I do. But I might be wrong; the lenses of his spectacles are thick and it is difficult to see exactly where he is looking.

I am sitting with the Chaplain when he comes; the Chaplain is facing me. The Choirmaster sits in the empty chair beside me without a word to either of us. My thoughts switch to ethnicity — that he might be responding in this manner because the Chaplain and I are Igbo. But there are indications that this is not so in the church as a whole. I quickly dispense with the thought, believing again that this is a university community and people in academia are not myopic.

"I think you should reconsider, Sir," the Chaplain says. He is wearing his reading glasses, which I associate with his nervousness. During Church Council meetings when he is proposing a change or defending a claim, he usually puts on his reading glasses. I cannot fathom why he is nervous and I am becoming irritated by his stance, his attempt to patronize the Choirmaster.

"Well, Sir, as I told Reverend Muna, I have been Choirmaster for more than twenty five years and we haven't needed any retreat. I don't even understand the rationale."

The Chaplain begins to explain how the retreat would serve an important, overarching purpose. The Choirmaster does not agree, but makes his own argument about the lengths to which he goes to ensure his choir is in good form.

"Your choir?" I blurt, a little above a whisper. He turns to me. Up till now I know he doesn't consider me a threat. He dispensed with me yesterday, and therefore I am no imminent trouble. I tell myself that I must prove him wrong.

"You say?"

"You used the words 'my choir.' I want to be sure that's what you said."

"I'm not sure those were the words I used."

"I heard you clearly. You said, 'my choir.' I heard you."

"I am sure I said '*the* choir.' You are mistaken."

"Well, I am not."

"Okay then. Whatever word I used, I do not agree that we should hold a retreat."

"You don't need to agree."

I keep my voice low so that our exchange does not become a quarrel, or my words offensive. If we maintain things at this level we could go on and avoid any serious damage. Yet I doubt the possibility of that.

"I am the Choirmaster."

"I am the Assistant Chaplain. He is the Chaplain."

"So what are you saying?"

"I am saying there is a hierarchy in this church."

Even the Chaplain looks at me with surprise, as he has never heard me speak in this manner. The Choirmaster is appalled; no one has stood up to him the way I am doing. I do not care.

"You can't expect me to do anything because of hierarchy."

"Then on what basis, Sir, are you going to do anything?"

"I have a PhD in music, Reverend Muna…"

"The Chaplain has a Masters in Divinity. He is pursuing a PhD in Religious Studies."

He shakes his head, but does not seem to give in. "So what are you saying?"

"I am saying your qualification is only important outside this church."

He looks at the Chaplain, then back to me and says, "You're insulting me. That is an insult!"

"You can take it whatever way you want to. We are to respect authority."

The Chaplain says, "Reverend Muna, please."

"Sir, you know I am saying the right thing."

"Keep your right thing to yourself," the Choirmaster says.

"Sir," I say, "if you do not hold that retreat, I'll see to it that things change in the choir. Do you think we all want to keep hearing the same songs for twenty five years?"

When I stand I see that the Choirmaster's head is bent and he is shaking it vigorously. The Chaplain says, "Reverend Muna," but I do not turn to him. When I am in my car I begin to smile, looking in the rearview mirror, expecting to see that my face has changed. It has not. I remember the days in Jos when I had the habit of washing my face. I remember Taibat's hand on my head. I keep smiling to myself, thinking that I have survived, again.

This time I have no limp. But things change.

Three

HELPER

I

She was not one of us.

She said her life was an early evening, or an early dawn, and she was going to leave before it was night or before it was morning. She gave you the feeling that you were inconsequential in the grand scheme of things, and that if you stood in her way you would disappear without any effort on her part.

She left her things with me and departed.

I remember her face made me think of a wild animal gone extinct and come back miraculously into existence. "I am leaving," she said. And the only thing I could do was nod. "These are my things," she said, pointing to a trunk. "Keep them for me." When I nodded again, she repeated, "Keep my things for me."

If you asked her what her plans were, like my father and mother had once done, she would say "I don't have any plans" or "I don't want to have any plans." When she came to me at midnight, sat by my bed, and asked me what I thought of the first four lines of the new song she was writing, I could say nothing because my eyes were filled with sleep. She would just stand up and leave. On one or two occasions she left her notebook with her lyrics behind.

Our mother said she was not one of us. "Ugo came out easily. She was easy for me, unlike you." But since Ugo left, my mother's voice has been subdued, hushed. Previously you could've heard her arguing loudly with Ugo about something. It could have been how she was dressed. Mother always thought her clothes were second-hand, masculine, unbecoming of a lady.

It was easy to guess Ugo's iconoclastic answer—the way her mouth would pout and her face would reveal the glorious, gracious show of defiance—"It's just the way I want to dress."

Unlike father, mother did not argue with Ugo so much. Ugo had father's face, or something close to it—she couldn't really be said to resemble anyone. Father did not really argue with her in the way mother did. He did not speak of her plans or her clothes. He looked at her as one would look at a witch, or as one would look at a man who appeared at his own funeral carrying his head under his arm. Because we sat each morning as a family to pray, to sing hymns, and to read from Our Daily Bread, it was easy to see father look at Ugo.

Ugo said to him once, "I really don't care what's on your mind." I feared she'd add, "Fuck you," or something as vulgar. If she had spoken those words to me, she would have added "Fuck you," given the frequency with which she spat the phrase when she leered at tradition. Yet, when she said this to father, he shook his head and returned his to his Bible, which he had begun to read too often since he'd come home one evening and announced that his job with British American Tobacco was over, telling us he'd just resigned. He would not tolerate tobacco; he would not encourage people to smoke and go to Hell.

The house sounded empty after he told us that. On that day, Ugo showed up wearing earphones. I thought she did not hear father. She did not have the expression we, mother and I, had—one of disappointment and submission. She looked beyond worry. But it was Ugo that stood up to father, challenging his decision. "That doesn't sound right." He looked at me and then turned to her. He looked at mother after he looked at Ugo, and turned to look at her again. I felt the walls speaking, saying that in no time they would all break down, considering the weight of everything, considering they were not built to shelter all the words and silence we used as weapons. Father said nothing to Ugo. He only looked at her. You know how silence can be more effective than words, how it is more deadly, how it is like a man appearing at the Spartan war without armor, with only his mouth.

Ugo walked out of father's silence that morning. It was impossible to argue with father; he had the ability to end a matter with his eyes. We knew this. You would hardly hear him argue with mother. But to walk away from him the way Ugo did was a fine way to argue with him. He hated incomplete arguments and hated losing confrontations. Ugo had a way of making his fight transient, winning when he had only begun the war.

She would ask all her questions. I was the conformist; she was not. She asked mother whether it wasn't "suicidal" to bear the burden alone. She told me that it was the most foolish thing she had ever heard. She told me it was a fact that Dad was being a fool, and that it was painful that he cared less about his foolery.

Ugo liked stones. In my earliest memory of walking to school with her, she would kick stones and look downward while she walked. We weren't twins; she was my elder sister, one year my senior. But, given that I had begun school at four and she at five, we ended up as classmates. She wasn't the smartest student. She was bright enough to do all the smart things that needed to be done. She never failed an exam. Even when I topped the class—term after term—she did not seem to bother, or compete. She always said, "Well done," with a face devoid of expression.

I liked the fact that she did not seem to want to compete. The story at home wasn't different—the unspoken feeling was that Ugo was doing badly. It was wrong for her to come below me in class. But all of this did not matter to her. We went to the same schools, even university. But she chose Law, and I chose English. There was a big battle at home—everyone thought it should have been the other way around. I could see my father's silence speaking of his disappointment. Only my mother asked, "Are you sure this is what you want? English?" and I said yes, thinking then that Ugo would have answered differently. She might've called their bluff. No one asked her if Law was right for her; with her you were never sure if you had asked the right question. At this point she was only the older child whose younger brother was doing well. She had not given us the idea that her life was an evening, that she was a Bedouin, a lone wanderer.

Everything changed with music.

In the long holiday after our third year, music discovered Ugo. We might all agree that music cannot discover, since it is sound and sound is the voice of nature; you should find music, not the other way around. But with Ugo it was different. She was an exception. The earphones that stayed permanently on her ears, the loud beats that came from behind her bedroom door, the records scattered on the floor of her room, and all the paraphernalia that came with the hybrid of a reggae star and a hip-hop artist established her life as the one whom music was destined to meet.

"This music is entering me. I feel full," she said to me two days before school resumed. I had come to ask her when we were leaving, to remind her that the new session was about to start. But all she talked about was her music. She drew close to me and put the right piece of her earphones in my ear. It was something by Jay-Z and Linkin Park. She held a notebook, and asked me to listen as she sang from it in tandem with the music in our ears. I could not mention the resumption of school. You know the feeling that comes with wanting to reach your reflection in the mirror and being unable to? So I walked out of the room and packed my things. I left Ugo at home.

The days passed quickly without Ugo. I did not miss her. But I would stop in the middle of something and my heart would skip and I would remember her. The words of the music she had shared stayed with me. The music that had been in our ears that day could not be lost, and I hated remembering how she had sung with reckless abandon, without a care for anything, anyone, custom, boundaries, and silence. I hated that I remembered exactly how the music in our ears had sounded:

Creativity weakens me as Smiles ache and
Hurt like laughter — Pushing through is all this is —
This time is time to end the wail

I could remember the way the words appeared on her yellow pad, her slanting handwriting. So I went home over a two-day holiday and I asked myself why I hadn't left before the holiday, if Ugo had mattered to me at all.

When she opened the door, mother said, "Your sister says she's through with school." I weighed the words, looked at my mother's face. There was something triumphant about her gossip, something you would see in the face of a scientist who discovered a new species. She had proven, it seemed, that Ugo was not one of us. We would not drop out of school — my father hadn't, my mother had not either, and I would not. We would not make passion out of music since music was a by-the-way thing, something done as a hobby; something done when one had studied hard and needed to ease off.

I went to her room. She hugged me. She had the smell of overripe oranges, the kind we'd ordinarily throw away. When she hugged me I held her limply. I held her like I shouldn't have held her, as though I would feel ashamed for having hugged my sister. There were records on her bed, as there had been when I left two months earlier. But this time it was easy to notice a difference: the family computer was now in her room.

"You know, I've been doing stuff on FruityLoops, recording my songs," she said. I looked at her more closely. She was wearing faded jeans and a worn t-shirt. Aside from her smell of overripe citrus, her clothing was the second most significant fact, especially if one wanted to verify the claim that she was not one of us.

The speakers attached to the computer came to life. Her voice became a person; the sound of a badly produced song, something done by an amateur, filled the room. But it was the opposite of a disembodied voice, a personality was singing. The music I heard was not music by a singer obliged to music; it was the music of a person to whom music was obliged. So hearing it felt like being hit by a swagger stick. Afterward you could not tell whether the effect was the result of the composer's notes, or the way they were sung, or something you sensed you knew about the history of the singer. There was the sound of a harmonica, or something close to it. It sounded like jazz, or blues, or bluegrass, everything all at once:

> *My life's work is to translate you*
> *I'll sing for you like a mockingbird*
> *But I'll be gone when you love*

I was carried away. The music was brief, only those lines sang in triplet. I had never heard a song like that, with only a stanza, sang three times. But then this was Ugo's song. I heard her saying to me, "I'll call it 'Mockingbird.' I want to make a record of twenty four short songs. People will listen to each song every hour. So that there's music throughout the day." I could have asked her what she'd name the album. But she was too excited for such a trivial question. I nodded. With Ugo it was sometimes difficult to do more than nod.

"I've completed ten songs. Fourteen left. I should finish before tomorrow." Again, I nodded. She went to the computer and clicked. Another sound wafted through the air. This time she sang along. You know how it is when you hear a song from a voice that cannot be undone, even by magic? Only super human powers could make Ugo leave herself. She sang with the confidence of a person who knew too much of the world, and who considered her role in it more important than any other's.

A streetcar shall
Carry me away
I shall give help
To a dead soul

The next day, she left her things with me and departed. The ceremony of her leaving was in the fact that there was no ceremony. We watched her leave. She dropped her trunk with me in my room. I followed her to the sitting room where my father was reading his Bible and my mother was punching the buttons on a calculator. Although she still wore her faded jeans, the worn t-shirt had been replaced by a clean, bright, Manchester United jersey. In the days when Ugo loved football, Manchester United had been her favorite club.

My father's silence argued with her, as usual. My mother looked up briefly from her calculator, then resumed her punching. Ugo established eye contact with me, looking behind in a passing glance. I bent my head. When I looked up, she was beside me. She whispered, "I finished only twenty three songs. I'll just record the last one in the street, with a tape recorder. There's music on the street, you know." I nodded. She hugged me. My hands remained limp by my sides, but hers pressed my back fiercely. I caught my father's unsupportive gaze, which let out his skepticism.

I left home for school the next day. With Ugo gone, there was a vestige of blandness in the house. And I hated the way my parents acted as though they had been freed. My father went to her room and took away the computer. It was then that I saw the CD. I knew what it was: Ugo's twenty three songs. I felt terrible because I knew I could not share the music with her—the music in her head would play only in her ears.

A few days after I returned, mother came to me at school; I met her car just as she arrived and saw that she had come with her shop's driver. He usually drove the truck when furniture had to be delivered. The car smelled of citrus. There were, indeed, oranges in her car.

"It's Ugo."

I could not ask her what was wrong; I thought I knew. I did not think of Ugo. I thought of mother's furniture shop, its showroom, the glass doors, and her salesgirls.

Her coffin was the size of a CD cover blown into egregious proportions. It was wide and short; not long and narrow. It must have been too big for her, misfit for her small frame. Her hands must've been folded across her chest, her small breasts. She must've have worn her beloved black socks, which she wore in heat and in cold. She must've entered the coffin unaware.

Mother and father stared at the coffin in silence. There was something worthy about mourning Ugo in silence, even something moral. If we had cried or wept loudly, it would have dishonored what Ugo had been. We could not mourn her the way we would have mourned any other.

Mother said a man had brought the news of her death: He said she had been hit by a truck; she had been crossing the road with earphones in her ear, with her music in her ears. It was difficult to locate her family. But on the back of her Manchester United jersey she had inscribed our surname: "Egwu." The man had asked around and found our house.

Her burial was a private affair—mother, father, mother's salesgirls. Then the man. When the priest finished the prayers, the man asked for an audience. He waved his hands in the air and started to weep. In between his sobs, with words that sounded choked but musical, he said, "She helped me. I was going to kill myself. She sang a song with me. I don't know what else to say."

I could have slapped him. I could have slapped him until he told me how she helped him. I could have told him he had no right to be helped by Ugo—he was not with me when Ugo had said, "Some of us are born for others. We might be born only to do one act of kindness." He was unqualified for Ugo's help.

There were many other things I could have done during her burial. If I had loved her enough, I could have carried her coffin to a private space known to me alone. I could have organized the launch of her album and called it "Twenty Four."

But, instead, one day, I opened the portmanteau that she had left with me. I poured the contents of the trunk onto my bed. I held each item—jeans, t-shirts, books, notepad. I smelled them; there was an aroma of overripe oranges. Then I put them back together. I threw the CD into the chest. Then I took her things outside and I burned them.

The night before I had played the CD over and over until my mother and father had joined me in the sitting room and we wept together. Ugo's music played in the background, all twenty three of her short songs.

I torched her things because the music in our ears did not stop playing.

II

A year after my sister's death, I rediscovered home.

Before I came to the point of rediscovery I was not indifferent about living in her shadows. Her death left me and my parents struggling to regain confidence in our fraternal capacities, as though she had left us with only detritus on which to stay afloat or else face drowning in the sea that was ourselves.

But I am wrong to presume that this coming-to-self was a shared effect of Ugo's death. I might be right to speak only for myself. In the days that followed her burial I locked myself in my room and tried to write songs. I did not enter her room in all the time I took to understand what her death meant. To enter her room would have been to stay in water while drowning, to hit my head on the wall when already bleeding.

It was my mother who dared to enter her room. When she came out she asked me, wide-eyed, "You burned some of her things?" When I nodded, she said, "I went to see if any of Ugo's things could make me forget." She seemed to want to say more, but she may have guessed I didn't see any sense in going into Ugo's room. For me it wasn't about forgetting. It was about having enough guts to forget that Ugo had not been one of us.

In a matter of days after her burial I began to distrust the capacity of my father and mother to forget that she was not one of us. Each time I considered the stoic sorrowfulness of my father's face, I figured that he would retain his conviction that Ugo was more or less a daughter who never became his. He would remain convinced that he couldn't get to her because she didn't conform to his standards. To him she was the one among us who failed to become one of us. My mother, who visited Ugo's room every day, was the one who wanted to have a daughter who was one of us. She did not understand that we had created for ourselves too many boundaries that did not exist for Ugo.

I packed my things and left. It was true I was returning to school to begin my final exams. Yet I perceived that behind me lay a lost fraternity with my father and mother. To uncover that relationship's terrain would be a difficult, if not impossible, adventure.

On the day when I left, my father asked, "You'll come back soon?" I didn't nod, couldn't. I saw that in his face there weren't any vestiges of the doctrinaire he had become since resigning his job, getting addicted to the study of the Bible, and being fed by my mother's business. He asked no question this time, "You'll come when you're through with your exams." I nodded because he seemed to affirm my return for his own sake, and that I wasn't necessarily inclined to act as he wished.

My mother gave a smile that sought to wrench my resolve, a smile that warned me that if I walked away she would forget me as surely as she was trying to forget Ugo. But I did not care. There are things you don't do for love.

Ugo once said that if she could keep her hands empty she would die a happy person. During the time I wrote my final exams, I felt haunted by my filled hands, by the fact that I was carrying too many selves within me that weren't me. I discovered, during that period, that I didn't know myself. I didn't have the knowledge that could be to me what music was to Ugo.

I say these things because, looking back, I am faced with the understanding that everything changes with the realization that being an exception is an exception in itself.

III

My mother advised us, when we were admitted to the University of Ife, to attend the interdenominational chapel she had attended as a student. In her time, she said, they had worshipped at the Agric Foyer, but she had heard that they had since moved to a building near the mosque, which was near the cemetery. All this was true. But she didn't advise us to join the choir—certainly not Ugo, while she was with us; certainly not me, not at the end of my stay in Ife, when I realized I had failed a course and would have to stay an extra year.

I failed by choice, by the conscious undoing of the possibility of success. I left the exam hall ten minutes after we'd been called in. It was like a looking glass accompanied me when I

115

sat, so that when I began to write I felt mirrored to the point of duress. I felt that if I continued nothing but the skeleton of my real self would leave the examination hall. So I walked out, caring less about the stares that seemed to dampen my shirt, stares that might have misunderstood my reason for leaving, guessing that I was sick. And when the supervisor asked me where I was going, I walked to him and said with a low voice, "I can't continue, really." I saw the spite in his face, the victorious speechlessness he expressed, his victory in knowing that by leaving I would fail the course.

All of this happened before I joined the choir.

Because the mystery of life is measured with subjectivity, I have not given much thought to my reasons for joining the choir. Standing while a hymn was being sung, the Sunday after I felt mirrored in the exam hall, I concluded that there was much intelligence in the lyrics of a song, that God gently whispered his wisdom in every line.

I began to exist thoughtlessly, acting without seeing the need to think or pre-enact, seeing myself as a passing ghost. I felt that joining the choir would draw me close to the uproarious intensity of God's whispers, and maybe then I would catch the substance of my shadow. Nothing other than this objective mattered, not my studies or anything else. I agree that I could have been senseless, beguiled by metaphorical and metaphysical inconsistencies. But that was the way I thought then.

Of course I did not return home after my exams. I still held a grudge against my parents for refusing to come to terms with Ugo's iconoclasm. I didn't believe they would understand my recent preoccupations. They had been my father and my mother for too long, and I wanted to know who I was without them.

So when my mother called to ask when I would return, I told her she shouldn't bother since I didn't know myself. As was usual of my mother she had no ready confrontational words. She exhaled loudly, said okay, and ended the call. My father, unlike her, asked me why. I told him a half-truth: that I had failed a course and needed to prepare for a rewrite. It was a half-truth because at that time I was yet to see my results, a half-truth because it was a convenient lie, a means to ward him off. He asked, "What do you mean you failed a course?" I said, unafraid of his anger for the first time in my life, "I mean I failed a course." I heard his pause, as though he was wondering how to handle my temerity. Then he said, "You failed? Just like that?" I said nothing. He told me, "You'll have to come home so we can talk, you hear me?"

I shook my head, half-expecting him to know that I had done so. There was a pause, then he ended the call. During the pause I thought I heard the turning of Bible pages. I wondered what my father was always searching for, maybe for himself, maybe for a specimen of that which he hoped to become.

And so I received weekly calls from my parents. My mother never suggested she wished for my return. She only asked the same question—"When are you coming?" My father was the one who cajoled and called my sanity into question. He threatened to stop my allowance, to disown me, to come to Ife and declare me mentally unfit. But these were things I was convinced he wouldn't dare do, not simply because he depended on my mother's financial support, but also because he was a man who cherished the sustainability of his ego and reputation.

A simple happening changed my mind. I used to attend the weekly rehearsals of the choir faithfully, given that I had joined at the beginning of my extra year. I had fewer academic commitments, and spent a lot of time learning to play the piano. Because of my commitment I was elected Youth Representative of the Choir.

It was a position invented by Mr. Lekan, the Assistant Choirmaster. He argued that, although the young members constituted a significant forty percent, our interests were overwhelmingly glossed over by the interests of older, non-student members. Nominations were requested and Sike, a girl who seemed to be interested in me and for whom I had no affinity, nominated me. Her friend seconded the recommendation and I was asked to rise. My opponent was Tiwa the Choirmaster's favorite for solos, but her voice did not sound extraordinary. She was disliked by most of the young members, perhaps because of her air of superiority. I won easily, pulling twenty three votes out of twenty seven.

The following week after rehearsals, Mr. Lekan asked me to go to the Choirmaster's office later that evening. I was supposed to deliver a letter to the Chapel Council requesting that a fund be set up for the younger members of the Choir to cater for their welfare needs. The last time I saw the Choirmaster he was driving away with Tiwa in his car.

That sight would not make sense until an hour later. I walked the distance to the Choirmaster's office in the Music Department, walking there on the footpath behind the church that led to the academic area of campus. While I walked, I evaluated how close I had come to ascertaining the tangibility of my life as a shadow. I realized that the music from the piano, which I was practicing every day, was becoming a major thrust of my life. I was at peace when I played, for the music seemed to arrange my emotions and personhood into a logical sequence. Each time I played I felt a rush of clarity to my head. While I walked I decided that when my mother called again, I would ask her to buy a piano for our house.

The Music Department buzzed with music-in-progress, amateur string instrumentalists, talking drummers, vocalists. The cacophony and hybridity of the music emanating from several rooms and open spaces in the music department brought a euphoric stillness to my mind. I stopped and for a moment I forgot non-musical affairs. It was when the drums became silent that I remembered my task. Before I moved I affirmed my resolve to get the piano for my house, thinking Ugo's room was best suited for it.

I knocked on the door labeled Dr. F. O. Ajuwon. There was no response. I knocked two more times. Then I turned the knob.

They formed a body, pressed together against the wall, the Choirmaster and Tiwa. Shocked, I quickly averted my gaze, and then retreated. But I was certain they'd seen me, confused as to why my knocks hadn't alerted them.

IV

The following week I arrived early, as usual, for rehearsals. Dr. Ajuwon sat in one of the pews at the back of the church, a stack of files beside him. I entered the chapel through the door at the rear, which made it easy for me to see him. I muttered a word of greeting to him, bowing my head lightly.

"I guess I can't eat my cake and have it too," he said to me. I nodded, without a clue as to what he meant and without looking at him.

"I'm resigning," he continued, fiddling with one of the files.

"Why, Sir?" I asked. I was standing close to him.

"I could lie to you, you know. I could tell you it's because the Chaplaincy is forcing me to hold a senseless retreat. But that would be a blatant lie." He avoided my gaze, but when he spoke next he looked directly at me, and I felt like a potato being mashed.

"I'm resigning because I am scared, you know, of what—of what you'll do." I was taken by surprise when I saw that his eyes were moist. I bowed my head, embarrassed on his behalf, surprised at his defensiveness, even more surprised that he expected me to act on what I'd seen.

119

"I know it's wrong what you saw. Just that I've had a very sad marriage. I shouldn't talk about this. I'll just resign before… er…word gets out."

After he spoke, I thought of my parents, wondering if theirs was a sad marriage too. All I said was, "I had no plans to say anything."

I walked out of the chapel thinking of how helpless my parents could be in the face of their reality, how they might have come to the point where they were clueless about anything different from the life they expected, or were used to. It was then that I rediscovered home, a timeless vestige that defied any expectation. I realized that my parents were all I had, that it mattered less if they understood that Ugo wasn't one of us.

I dialed my mother's number, and when she called my name with surprise in her voice, I stammered something about the piano. I told her I was coming home.

Four

THE MUSEUM OF SILVER LIGHTS

I

She was gone before I remembered. Her voice had sounded like the pouring of water into an empty cup; her eyes had seemed as though they could see things yet to be. Her life always seemed to be on the verge of happening. She used to talk of doing something. Even when my elder brother was alive and laughter bounced off the walls of our house, and music was an early morning gift.

There was a mahogany plank fixed to the front door of my brother's house. On it he had inscribed, "Because it is mine" underneath the words "Peace Villa," the name of the house. The letters were painstakingly engraved and cut deep in the wood. Even before he died she had spoken of changing those words to "Because it is ours." She was my brother's wife, see.

She was tall and effortlessly athletic, and there was a gaze in her eyes that was alert yet vulnerable. Her complexion, which I considered peculiar, appeared to roam through shades—she could seem dark-skinned today and albino-yellow tomorrow. And she spoke of the Museum of Silver Lights. I heard her argue with my brother once about turning the hallway of his brick house into the "first phase" of the museum. He asked her in a mocking tone what she'd keep in the museum. She told him the word "museum" derived from the word "muse" and that it could mean "a place for muse."

My brother, in his usual dissatisfied manner, asked, "What do you mean?"

And she told him, "I want to keep old photos in the museum."

My brother shook his head and looked at her in a way that spoke of her longstanding madness. Her eyes met mine, then looked away.

My brother died the next day in a big fight. He was a car dealer. His was, by all standards, the biggest car shop in Jos. The fight had erupted two shops away from his warehouse. It went the way all big fights go. His shop was burned. He went with his shop.

Her crying was the least pronounced. Our neighbors shed more tears than she did. They spoke to me in her stead. But even in my brother's days they would have talked to him to talk to her—even if she sat with them in the living room. When a group of Igbo men came to commiserate, they considered me old enough and talked to me while she sat with us. If you had not known, you'd have thought she was an apparition sitting in the living room while we mourned.

The Igbo community in Jos staged a protest against my brother's death—on the manner in which the authorities had treated the incident. It was a clear case of ethnic hegemony. On the morning of the demonstration, I asked her if she was going to join. She shook her head and asked me if I had eaten. She was the kind of person who tied two unrelated things together—a protest and a meal, a death and a museum. So I wasn't surprised when she asked me next, "You think I can start the museum now?"

I could have said I didn't think museums were *started*, or that it was an inappropriate thought given the circumstances. But instead I said, "Yes." And when she nodded, smiled, and rubbed my shoulder, I said "Yes" again.

I did not join them in the protest. I heard that only ten men showed up, and that they had called it off when no one else joined.

She replaced the mahogany plank that read "Peace Villa" with one inscribed with "The Museum of Silver Lights," and underneath the words she added, "Because it is ours."

Yes, she had confronted my brother about the words he had inscribed on the plank. When I visited earlier she talked about the phrase in a way that showed she had spoken about it before. "You can't just declare that this house is yours. If nothing, there are other people living here."

My brother said, without turning to her, "Leave me alone."

She pursed her lips and looked up, then shook her head. She walked away from him. I wondered why she spoke of the words on the plank—I thought she shouldn't be bothered about such little things.

One day she called me. She had come home earlier with photographs in silver frames. She had covered the single bulb in the hallway with a silvery screen. Now she had driven nails into the hallway wall and hung the photographs in a crisscross manner. They were photos of my brother and her on different occasions. She spoke of each photograph as a guide would do in a museum—"We took this in Abuja" or "He had just come back from China, at the airport." But I was angry. She hadn't invited me over to help put up the photographs. She said, "We'll fill the house with more photographs. Maybe we can open it up to the public. They would see his face."

I walked away from her. She spoke of my brother as though he had had no mind of his own.

While she slept I took down all the photographs—all twenty three of them. I carried them outside the house and broke each of the photographs into bits with a stone.

In the morning when I woke, she was gone. There was a white sheet of paper on the table in my room. She had started to write something, but canceled the thought. I could see where the pen had torn the paper while she scratched off the words she'd written.

The Igbo community in Jos told me they were going to stage a protest against the manner of her death. I told them it was unnecessary. Their spokesman, a reverend who kept dreadlocks, asked me why. I told him I was going back to my parents in Ibadan. That was all.

"Is that all?" he asked.

I said, "Yes. That's all."

I told him that if he wanted to do something for her memory, he should have something important written on her grave. He asked what. I told him "Because you were ours." Then I told him no. He should have them inscribe "Museum of Silver Lights" instead. He frowned. I told him to call off the epitaph idea entirely.

On the day she was buried someone came with a handwritten invitation he claimed she had given him. It read, "Please attend the opening of the Museum of Silver Lights." And our address was written on it.

They said she had been hit by a car while distributing her handwritten invitations.

II

I often dreamed of an empty room with light bulbs covering its ceiling. In my dreams I watched the lit room from a distance, usually unable to go in. Sometimes this dream happened when I was awake. I knew then that it was fixed in my memory; I knew my dreams by heart. I had come to that point when I was the one who determined what I dreamed about, what I made-believe. And this capacity, this ability to stretch myself to such lengths, did not come by chance.

After my sister-in-law died, my parents came to Jos and took me away. They decided for me. I was going to Ife; I was going to study law. There are times when I assume I was brainwashed. In my earlier stubbornness I had not conceived that my parents could prevail over me. Yet, in a matter of time, it became my own wish to study law in Ife; I made my dream. There were so many things that had happened—my brother and his wife, their deaths—that my grasp on the dividing line between what was real and what wasn't had become blurred. In circumstances of this kind, you would ask yourself whether you were certain of what was and what wasn't—and when you thought you had found the answer, the question would present itself again.

There were other reasons why I chose to attend the chapel, aside from the fact that a classmate whom I admired had invited me. She was a girl I thought I loved, until I told her and she said we would spoil things if she accepted. So, even though she stopped attending the chapel and I began to see her with another boy from another church on campus, I kept attending the chapel. There was something about the size of the compound that intimidated me, made me believe that I couldn't understand its complexity even if I tried. The hall could probably sit about five thousand, but fewer than five hundred were regular members.

I joined the Youth Fellowship. On my first Sunday, Tutu—that was her name—gave me a copy of *Seeds*, a monthly publication by the Youth Fellowship. In my first year I decided that I wanted to write poetry. Seeing that *Seeds* had no poetry, I considered joining the editorial team, so that I could contribute some poems. I asked Tutu to introduce me to the editor. His name was Jackson; he was in his final year and was bored: editing *Seeds* had become humdrum. In another two years I had become the editor of the paper.

Oko Egwu wrote for *Seeds* occasionally. He told me after a Youth Fellowship meeting that he wanted to write a short piece about the choir, or that it would be better if I wrote it. I told him it was going to be difficult, seeing as we had only a little over a week before the next issue would be released.

He told me why he wanted me to write it.

"You think it's going to be sensible?" I asked him.

"Well, let's try."

I shook my head, understanding the import of what he was asking. "We're really inconsequential here," I told him.

"Really?" he asked. I took it to mean he was asking, "You want it to remain so?"

Before he left Ife, Jackson had introduced me to a friend of his, a medical student. He said that his friend was a good poet, the best he knew, and that while poetry bored him, his was an exception. So he introduced me to his friend, a certain Damilola Ajayi. I asked Damilola for his poems on the evening when Oko Egwu spoke of writing about the choir, and he searched in the bag he was carrying for something he had scribbled that morning.

I decided to use Damilola's poem for the coming issue of *Seeds*. I had typed it on my laptop, but when I decided to write about the Choir it became likely I would do away with the poem, for space. Yet, there were lines in Damilola's poem that answered the question Oko had asked me: "You want it to remain so?" It was like the feeling of not knowing what was real and what was false, not knowing when you had caught a plague or when you were dying from natural causes. The lines from the poem were:

The story is a tragedy
But it's a story nonetheless.

Oko's objective was to get the young people in the choir, which he happened to head, to agree with the Assistant Choirmaster's proposition to hold an election during the forth-coming retreat. *Seeds* was due to come out two Sundays before the retreat. I told him he was relying on a fluke, that not many people took our work in *Seeds* seriously.

He looked at me. I understood his concerns. It was surprising even to me that I edited *Seeds* but did not believe in my work. It was surprising that my life seemed to comprise of things I didn't completely believe in—commonplace, lackluster elements gave form to my life. Despite having accepted to write about the choir, I did not trust myself or my writing—Damilola had once told me a writer's life was a hybrid of moments of intense doubt and moments of stellar brilliance.

I called Oko when *Seeds* arrived. There was a fight in my head even before he said he wasn't sure we could distribute the paper. It was the first time he read what I wrote—our schedule had been tight. I smiled and asked him why.

"This is dangerous, Christian."

I knew he was afraid but I asked myself if I was any different. We sat in a small room that served as an office for the Youth Fellowship, filled with musical instruments, a computer, a small collection of Christian literature, and undistributed past editions of *Seeds*. I called him because I wanted him to see what I had written. He worsened what I felt by saying what he said.

"That's impossible. You know it."

"Are you ready for what will happen?" he asked.

I smiled again. "You expect trouble when you are speaking the truth."

He chuckled, nervously. "Is this the truth, Christian? Agreed, it might be our truth, because we want to believe it is. But there's the truth of the older people, and they won't fancy our truth, I tell you."

I held his shoulder, showing affection I felt was unnecessary, and said, "It doesn't matter whose truth it is—"

"It matters!" he retorted sharply. But that was all he said; he looked crestfallen, a look that showed he was leaving things unsaid. He walked out. I wanted to call him back, talk to him and convince him that I was not as scared as he was. But I could only see his hunched shoulders, the way his body seemed to sag when we talked, and I knew my body wasn't different. It was sagging and unsure.

There was man in the chapel, Dr. Addo, who always sat in the first pew. He was considered eccentric and unreasonable, but he had a PhD in electrical engineering and lectured in the same department. His students said he cursed in class, called the Yoruba gods of thunder and lightning on all those who taught them that it was unnecessary to memorize whole textbooks or substantial parts of his lecture notes. But in the chapel, mostly during the sermon, he raised his hand in agreement, asserting himself in a way that made me think he was putting an end to doubts of his irrelevance.

I saw him walk up to the Choirmaster just after the church service ended. He walked as though on fire, casting his legs in front of him with absolute certainty. The chapel was still filled with members who were making small talk. I stood behind, some yards from the Choirmaster, making myself look busy, but actually intending to eavesdrop. I heard Dr. Addo saying, "Did you see this?" over and over to the Choirmaster. The Choirmaster was surrounded by choristers, who had stayed on after the service. Then Dr. Addo stopped asking the question and began to tear *Seeds* into shreds, bit by bit, littering the chapel. There was now a substantial number of choristers standing by as he tore up the newsletter. Some members of the chapel walked to where he stood.

Two minutes later I heard Dr. Addo say, "Where is that Christian Ike? Does anyone know him?" A part of me wanted to walk to him and surrender myself to any consequence they intended to deliver. But I considered that foolhardy. I walked quietly out of the building, hoping that nobody saw how I escaped from the limelight, or whatever it was that could have happened if I had confronted the professor.

I tried to think about whether it would be trite to put that issue of *Seeds* in a glass and hang it in my room in school. Perhaps it would be better to take it home, where there were reminders of the life I had lived in Jos—the life my brother's wife had lived, the lights she had seen, her botched Museum of Silver Lights.

As I walked I wondered what Oko was thinking, if he had gotten what he wanted, if he had not given himself the excuse that he did not know what he wanted. I imagined there were young people who would be stirred by what I wrote, and I imagined there were those who would disagree, for whom the choir had no need for change. And there might be those in between, for whom nothing was right or wrong—for whom all that was necessary was the continued functioning of the choir, irrespective of what I wrote, or did not write.

I heard my name being called. I stopped and saw that it was Oko. He was panting from running, but he was smiling. I wanted to ask him why he was smiling, but I can only dream that he had dreamed my dream of an empty room, whose ceiling was covered with light bulbs, waiting for us to enter, awakened, dreaming no more.

Five

THE SOUND OF THINGS TO COME

I

She awoke into the wonder of ordinariness. The things she began to see right there as she left her bed, things disguised by the lightless room, struck her in a manner they never had before. She had the room memorized by heart and could recreate the setting from memory—a bedside lamp on the cabinet by her side of the bed, a pile of books on the cabinet by her husband's side, the wardrobe at the corner with white doors protecting clothes and shoes, a photograph on their bed's headrest, other items whose positions she could mentally pinpoint. She was confused as to why she felt haunted by the blandness of it all—the fact they had been acquired and were now owned. She was possessed in the middle of that night by a nightmarish suddenness, an unfamiliar pang that could not be named.

She stood up, glanced at her husband and paused to hear his quiet snore, then walked away from their lightless room, easily finding her way in the dark. In the sitting room she stood and imagined the space as she knew it—nothing had changed in two years of marriage—how the efforts they had put in when they had just got the house still defined the room's paraphernalia. It was the same map of Africa that covered most of the wall to her right, a large map Edwin, her husband, had got a student in the Fine Arts Department to sketch. At the time it hadn't bothered her. They had decided the living room would be jointly furnished—she busied herself with purchasing the rest of the furniture while Edwin worried about the map. The items she brought in, especially the chairs, were gifts from retiring professors, her mentors—an old man and his wife who craved frugality. At that time the furniture, bought originally in the early Eighties, appealed to her as leftover history, and so their plainness hadn't mattered. Now that same historicity was unappealing, even when she looked at the chairs in the darkness.

She faced the map and in it she saw all her husband's ambition. Edwin dreamed of a road trip across Africa, overland from Cairo to Cape Town, and often spoke of that quest as outranking the depth of the world, a depth that meant an intangible quality of tourism. She felt tempted to switch on the lights, to see the map clearly, for she wasn't sure if she had imagined it correctly. But she wasn't ready to stand in a lit room. Even more importantly, she didn't think seeing the map would make her feel less plagued by ordinariness. So what, she thought, if there's a larger-than-life map of Africa in this room? So what!

Before she sat down she remembered the glass shelf adjacent to the map—also a gift from a retiring professor. When he gave it to her he said he was too old for glamor and she probably needed it more. She succumbed to his ascetic imprudence. There was nothing spectacular about the shelf, aside from its showiness. And this was the quality that she and Edwin leveraged. The shelf was two-tiered: the photos on one tier and a handful of books (Dostoyevsky, Achebe, Rushdie, Eco, Coetzee), a Yoruba Bible, and an Igbo Bible on the other. What made her mind tired of reimagining the nature of the shelf in the darkness was what she considered a glassy irreverence—the covering of their important things behind glass. She sighed. There was no point to the glass, after all.

What had brought her to this point in time where she could clearly view the ordinariness of their lives? She couldn't tell, although she spent another thirty minutes speculating. She wasn't a restless person, as far she could tell. Up to that point, her life consisted of long-ranging ambitions, the kind that made a person remain in one place for decades. It was the kind of homeliness that made one think of studying for a PhD in the same school where one obtained a Master's degree. But this night, in a manner she couldn't explain, she visited her house in a fit of wonder; she was bored with the routine of seeing the same things, sleeping with the same man, being his wife, thinking of having his child.

The wonder of ordinariness was an illogical phrase, she knew, but she kept repeating it in her mind, rummaging through memory for a similarity with something she'd read, some profound novel, an unforgettable character perhaps. Yet it was difficult to speculate courses of action—maybe leaving, she thought, and then she thought again...maybe staying. The most trivial option would be to rearrange the sitting room, confer on the ordinariness an element of distinction. But that seemed an ephemeral solution. She thought how "their" was fast becoming a difficult word to use—she feared she was folding into herself, performing an irremediable act of becoming.

Later that night, asleep on their sofa, Mo woke up to a shout. After the fog of sleep drifted away, she recognized that it was the voice of Beam, her sister. She stood up and waited for a few seconds to be certain it was a known voice. Then she sprinted to her sister's room.

Her husband had gotten there before her. They watched Beam twist in her sleep, screaming, "No, No!" The light was on—Beam liked to leave the lights on while she slept—and so it was easy to see the horror as it flitted across her sister's face. Mo turned to Edwin and saw the surprise, then the shock, on his face. They were both new to this. In another minute the screaming subsided, and a few seconds later all that was left was a frown on Beam's face. Mo thought of the word "knotted," in the aftermath of the screaming. Beam's eyes were now open, but her face retained a certain knottiness. Only her eyes did not betray any strangeness; they were the eyes of someone coming awake—like a newborn, one coming into existence for the first time, as though she was a character unaware of a role. In another moment Mo saw Beam's eyes take in her surroundings. The blank slate of her mind was soon filled with awareness. Beam's eyes met hers, but Mo did not let the gaze linger; she looked above her sister's head, turning to Edwin. He was transfixed and speechless.

Knowing him, Mo understood that his sense of practicality had been assaulted—he was a fix-it junkie, as she once called him, one who was plagued with the need to see the resolution of events, enveloped with the consciousness of logic.

Beam said, "I had a dream."

Mo's first thought was, so what—but then she felt selfish. "What was the dream about?" Edwin asked. Beam did not readily answer; she closed her eyes. The knotty look stayed fixed on her face. Mo kept thinking of "knotty" and "fix-it junkie"—it was her disease, she recognized, a bout of word-mania in the unlikeliest of times.

"Abimbola?" Mo called finally, feeling that only the pronunciation of her sister's full name would suffice.

"I'm here," Beam answered.

"What's up?" Edwin asked.

"It was a bad dream."

"Is that why you shouted?" Mo asked.

"I shouted?"

"Yes," Edwin said, then sat beside Beam on the bed. Mo stood where she was, aware of the torn negligee, her sister's lustrous dark skin, and the concern on Edwin's face. She knew it was something she shouldn't think about—she wondered about both of them alone together, whether Edwin was ever tempted. The day before she would have readily dismissed such thoughts, feverishly mining testimonies of her husband's fidelity. But that

night, after the feeling of ordinariness she had felt and now
Beam's dream, she sensed her mind shrugging.

"What was the dream about?" Edwin asked again.

Beam hesitated, and Mo knew she wouldn't tell. She suspected her sister had forgotten the upsetting dream.

"I cannot remember. But if I think some more I will
remember."

"Okay then," Mo said, "tell us when you remember."

Mo was suddenly and inexplicably afraid of the consequences of illogicality. How could a dream that came with
screaming mean anything? With what instruments could one
measure the relevance of dreams, their significance on real, every-
day existence? It seemed like a sci-fi novel, though she had never
completed any. The closest she had come was Huxley's *Brave New
World* and Wells' *The Country of the Blind*. Both books were like
dreams. The ephemeral quality of those sci-fi novels gave her
something to think about during the moment of silence. After
she said, "Tell us when you remember," neither Edwin nor Beam
said anything. She figured they were probing logicality as well:
fix-it junkies.

Well, she thought, *I'm not a fix-it junkie; I traffic in subtleties.*
"I'll see you guys later," she said aloud, walking out.

Mo's schedule, now that she was through with lecturing her graduate students, consisted mostly of teaching second- and third-year
literature students. The morning after her foray in the wonder of
ordinariness and Beam's dream, she had three classes — one at 9:00
a.m., another at 11:00 a.m. There was another that afternoon at 3:00
p.m., for which she did not want to show-up, African American
Literature. Only nine students had signed up that semester, and
that was a record. For previous sessions the number was half as
much. Although it was her favorite subject, given the books she'd

recently added to the reading list (*The Known World, The Bluest Eye, The Color Purple*), the same feeling of having a bland routine that had pervaded her consciousness the night before made her feel her favorite class would be boring.

After her 11:00 a.m. class, she felt she needed to write an email. This left her smiling. An email? And to whom? The only thing clear to her was the body of the message; when she felt prompted to write, a sentence from Colm Toibin's novel *The Story of the Night* flashed through her mind: "We saw nothing, not because there was nothing, but because we had trained ourselves not to see."

She walked to her office, one she shared with Mr. Adaraniwon, now in Wales for his PhD. His absence was an undisguised blessing, and she often hoped he wouldn't return. While she walked a few students greeted her, but she responded only in passing, almost bumping into Professor Segun, whose office was next to hers. She apologized—her vision was blurred by the words in her head…the email she felt compelled to write.

She wrote the letter before she had figured the words for the subject line or the addressee. It read:

While leaving my class this morning I thought of writing an email. I do not write creative stuff—although my life and career have depended mostly on the imaginative. William Carlos Williams wrote, "The imagination will not down. If it is not a dance, a song, it becomes an outcry, a protest. If it is not flamboyance, it becomes deformity; if it is not an art, it becomes a crime." And then, while I wondered about the rationality of imagining a written email that outlined my recent foray into blandness, I recalled Colm Toibin.

I am serious about this, although my sister's strange behavior last night is threatening to hush me into silence. What could I in this context be silent about? Well, in the hours after I woke in the middle of the night speculating ordinariness, I have given much thought to companionship.

I find it a waste. No, I shouldn't say "find" as though I have come to a conclusion. I should probably use "finding" because this is a quest. It is imagination in motion — a "dance," a "song."

So I guess I have seen nothing all this while because I have trained myself not to see. How could one train oneself to see? If I could train myself to see, I feel I would become whole. As things are I am beginning to see. Perhaps clarity will come soon. And does this suppose that I would become insensitive to illogicality, to my sister's strange screams and dreams? Maybe clarity is akin to logic — just maybe.

Kind regards,

Moyosore

She shut her eyes and figured a subject and a recipient. It was the kind of email that was sent as a bulk message, given its collective undertone. Then she remembered him. Peter had come to Ife for a conference a year earlier—he had been, at the time, teaching early African literature in the Obafemi Awolowo University, Ile-Ife. The conference had been organized by her Department of Literature in collaboration with the School of African and Oriental Studies in London, where Peter was now installed. After the conference he spent another week, mostly in her office, working on a paper. She guessed that it was an excuse to be with her—she told him she was married, but in an intriguing and bold way he still flirted with her. She did not push him away because she saw that he didn't want sex, never brought it up or suggested going that far. It was the first time she met a man whose flirtation was premised on the sexiness of her love for literature, for words and imagination. They spent hours discussing the limits of literature, the bliss of phrases, how wordlessness often sufficed, and artistic dissidence. Once, at around 7:00 p.m., while he prepared to leave for the conference center's guesthouse, he whispered in her ear, "We could retain these literary ties forever." Then he chuckled and hurriedly shoved his things into his bag, leaving her standing where she was. When he was out of her office, she smiled.

It was that smile she remembered when she decided she'd send the email to him. So she added "Dear Peter" at the beginning of the message. She didn't have difficulties getting a subject. His words, which had not meant much at the time—"We could retain these literary ties forever"—acquired a new resonance. She had always thought they suggested endless permanence. But now a different twist of its meaning accosted her. There was a transience she could not explain.

She wrote "leaving" in the subject line, hoping that in a few hours she would understand the dynamics of that word.

Mo called one of her students and canceled the 3:00 p.m. class, deciding to return home. Beam met her at the door and Mo smiled what she knew was a fake smile. Beam greeted her with a wider smile, taking her handbag. When she entered the sitting room Edwin was there, holding a plate of jollof rice, sitting and facing the over-sized map.

"Hey," Mo said.

"Hey," Edwin replied. She went to where he was and sat beside him, looking at the jollof rice he was eating. She was tempted to shove a few spoonfuls into her mouth, but she was equally tempted not to disturb his meal.

"You want some?" Edwin asked.

"No thank you," she said.

"Probably for the best. We burned it."

At the mention of "we" Mo turned to look at Beam, who was sitting in the dining area, also eating. Her sister had the look of a sailor contemplating a faraway shore.

"B," Mo called to her.

"Yeah, I'm here."

"I didn't ask if you are here. You served him burned rice?"

"I fell asleep. I'm sorry."

Mo turned to look at Edwin. She married him, among other things, for his nonchalance, the surge of okayness he possessed. There were few men, she knew, who didn't have anger lurking in their insides, a general dissatisfaction with the scheme of things. He was not the kind of man that thrived on ego. He was mellow... too mellow, now that she thought of it.

"Really, Mo, considering what she's seen, you shouldn't bother her."

"I'm scared she'll forget more than a pot of rice. I'm scared she'll forget everything." Mo said this to spite Beam, but she recognized that it had a tinge of collective spitefulness.

"You should be asking what she has seen."

"Well, what has she seen?"

"Beam, tell her."

After a brief hesitation, her sister told her the dream of the night before, as she recalled it. Although this was the second time it was being told, Mo felt it was being remodeled for her sake. Wasn't that a selfish, egoistical thought?

Beam's dream was a dream of gunshots and two dying men. A crowd, Beam said, was gathered in one instance. And in another instance the crowd had dispersed. She was with the crowd. She heard gunshots, but could not tell who was shooting, or at what. There were two men ahead of her and she was running to catch up with them. She saw them fall, bleeding, then she stopped running, turning to see a gun by her side. It seemed to have been there all the time. She ran to them, screaming as life ebbed from them. They died in unison. Beam said that was as far as she could remember.

Mo could feel Edwin's eyes on her, peering to see if she could make anything of the dream. She could not—indeed, she didn't feel as though there was anything to be made out of it.

"I've told her," Edwin said, "It's only a dream."

"That's not how I feel about it," said Beam. She was not looking at them, but above them, possessed, it seemed, by a transcendent worldview.

"Well, B, how do you feel about it?"

She took a few moments. "There seems to be a larger meaning, as if it's a revelation."

Mo thought of two things—Edwin's fervency in church, he had become an usher, and Beam's growing interest in prayer. Mo felt she was the impious one of the trio; although she attended church, she wasn't interested in what she termed celestial spiritualness. She came to God as a simple, wanting human, but decided that if God or his spokespersons demanded more than she could give, she'd recoil into secularity. So far, not much had been demanded of her. Edwin wanted her to become an usher as well, but she told him she was fine with regular Sunday attendance, even more than satisfied with the rigid worship pattern of the church they attended.

"A revelation? What does that mean?"

Edwin chuckled when she said this. Mo heard Beam's sigh. She knew there wouldn't be any response. Mo considered that she could be hurting her family with her spitefulness. But there was a boldness that accompanied spite, and she had it. She looked at her husband and he looked at her. His chuckle had become mischief on his face, daring her to revel in her spite, if it was worth it. Yet, knowing him, she perceived he probably wasn't daring her, that perhaps he was daring himself to dare her.

Beam's sigh echoed in her head, haunting her, making her feel guilty. She recalled what she had written, "My sister's strange behavior last night is threatening to hush me into silence." Why did she consider Beam's dream strange, even antagonistic? Shouldn't she be bothered about the implications of the "revelation"? Mo heard her own skepticism and feared what it was making her become. "A revelation? What does that mean?"

She stood and looked at the clock. It was only a quarter to three. She felt like returning to her office, reading a book, continuing a paper. That was what it came down to—herself, her ambitions.

"Guys, I'll just go back to the office," she said, avoiding Edwin's gaze. She saw that Beam nodded. She wanted Edwin to ask her to remain, but he said, "I'm out in ten minutes." Sometimes she wished they would oppose each other, that he wouldn't adore her like he did and accept her insensitivities so simply. That evening she was moved to tears, wondering how she had remained a wife for two years and a sister for much, much longer.

Back in her office, Mo checked her email and found Peter's reply. It wasn't a surprise that he responded early, even though their correspondence since he left Nigeria had been scarce. In a year they hadn't exchanged ten emails. When she thought of it, before she wrote him with "leaving" in the subject line, she felt it was a mutual wordlessness that assuaged their need to reach out to each other, the feeling that no number of emails would speak the volume of words that could be spoken.

His email was as impersonal as hers. She was, as before, drawn to a man who understood her so well, as though there was some force in the universe that made them genderless twins, entwined despite the limitations their racial difference conferred.

Dear Moyosore,

I can relate to "illogicality" but "ordinariness" is not my specialty. I will, however refer you to Night Train to Lisbon, pages 214 to 220. I think those pages contain the most important lines of that book, and I hope you agree with me.

You will recall Craig Owen: "Perhaps it is in this project of learning how to represent ourselves—how to speak to, rather than for or about others—that the possibility of a 'global' culture resides." Although he was speaking of, should I say, intercultural dialogue (which my friend Kwasi Wiredu has aptly written about) I believe that one cannot dialogue "without," if there's no inner dialogue.

These things do not exist in the realm of logic. Just like your sister's dream. We should, necessarily, approach things of that sort with constrained skepticism.

Ah, I write too long. Mercier's Night Train is a good read.

(Incidentally, I have been appointed Director of the Pascal Mercier Centre in the University of Bern. If you have any reasons to think of "leaving" Nigeria, Switzerland could be an option.)

Peter

Mo read the email again and again, discovering possible extensions of each word, thinking less of what limits they imposed. She knew it was her imagination; what scared her were the possibilities of the thoughts she'd begun to have, the implications of lusting after extraordinariness. A few more re-readings and the words in the email blurred. She stood up, feeling unaware. The email had numbed her into uncertainty about a simple matter: whether to return home or remain in her office. She checked her watch; it was getting late. She tried to remember when she had left Edwin and Beam eating, but couldn't. So she sat down and tried to find clarity.

She recalled Pascal Mercier, his book. Standing up immediately she tried to remember where she had kept it—Peter, being obsessed with Mercier, had given her a copy. But at that time reading it hadn't appealed to her, more so because at the time she wasn't interested in European writers. Now Peter seemed to suggest that Mercier held the key to her heart, the key to finding herself. She scanned the bookshelf in her office; it wasn't there. *The Night Train to Lisbon* must be at home.

Mo walked to her car uncertain of what she would find in the book and whether it would bring her closer to understanding what plagued her, what Peter had summed up in two words: illogicality, ordinariness.

Beam was asleep when she returned; Edwin was not in. She was sure he would be at his office. He, like her, was at the stage of writing his PhD thesis—something on double descent in African societies. He scarcely shared the details of his research with her, nor did he draw her into his anthropologic world; not that she was disturbed by that. Yet now that she felt in need of a change, a magical swipe at stability, she wondered if talking about double descent could spark in her an allure for the uncommon. She instinctively checked on Beam, seeing that her sister was sleeping in the negligee from last night. It was difficult to ascertain if it was torn from her twisting the night before, and more difficult to discern any anomaly. How could she expect, she thought, to investigate the subjectivity of sleeping, of dreaming? How could one tell only by looking the wanderings of a sleeper in dreamland?

Mo sighed at the impossibility of it all.

She walked to her room, opened the wardrobe, and pulled out a drawer. If she still had a copy of Mercier's novel she would find it here. After a few moments of searching through books she didn't read often, she found it, and what struck her first was the motion on the front cover. What she considered "motion" was a photograph of a man in dark clothing and a woman in a bright red gown, both carrying umbrellas, both walking. Was this the person into whom she was turning? A person in motion? A person shielding herself from the elements? What elements?

Mo sat on her bed and turned on the bedside lamp, gathering her legs on the bed with her shoes on. When her back was rested against the headboard she thought of Beam and her torn negligee, and the peace that didn't seem absent from her sleeping form. She remembered Peter had said pages 214 to 220. Against her better judgment (What was the point in reading only part of a book?) she leafed through until she came to 214. The italicized sentences attracted her because italics, as she once joked, were the slanting voice of higher reasoning. When she opened books that contained "slanting voices" she listened to what they had to say.

After reading the first sentence on page 214 she stood and went to her drawer, seeking something to write on. She found a notebook, then a pen. *Life is not what we live; it is what we imagine we are living*. She felt stung. She looked at the words again, as though to see if they would become winged and fly away from her. What stunning profundity, she thought. If Mercier's words were true it meant the real deal was not the routine life she lived with her husband and Beam, but the one she could imagine. She conceived all sorts of possible imagined lives—one in Bern as a Pascal Mercier Fellow, for instance, apart from her husband, a life that was not conjoined, a life that did not demand the hassles of being a crutch. Mo allowed her imagining of that life to linger.

She fell asleep without intending to. Mercier's words became her dreams.

Around midnight, when she was awakened by her sister's shouts, Mo felt a clarity she hadn't felt the last time. It was the clarity of knowing that her sister's dream did not sound sensible, was a disputable "revelation." She stood up when she saw Edwin hastily leave the room. There was no hurry in her head; she saw no point in according strategy to an occurrence that traveled on the threshold of intangibility. The screams continued, but after a minute could no longer be heard—by which time Mo had sat back on the bed and switched on the bedside lamp. Was it insensitivity, she wondered, to crave for more lines from Pascal Mercier while one's sister was plagued with an ungraspable dream?

Human beings can't bear silence; it would mean they would bear themselves.

Beam was Mo's only sister. Mo had assumed a parental role as soon as Beam was born, a duty she had lapsed into without choice, because their mother died during labor. Their father, who was then in the cocoa business, controlled a substantial fortune and had lavished this wealth on his daughters to gloss over his grief. Mo knew that her father never became whole again after having lost his wife without warning. She wasn't sure if it was the death or the forced responsibility that had made him an unwholesome, needing man. At age eleven Mo became Beam's mother, and she felt that after twenty-three years, she still was.

But how could she, having a history of motherhood, choose to remain on her bed with Mercier while her sister screamed and wallowed in intangibility? It made no sense to her—this was the point at which she knew something in her was pulling away, when she couldn't speedily respond to the demands of responsibility.

"You're reading a book?" It was Edwin's voice.

"No, not really. I was reading it earlier."

"I see."

He sat beside her on the bed. She looked at his unsmiling face and felt he was right to be vexed with her, and yet she also felt that there was no point in seeking to understand his confusion. Usually in anger he was silent, and usually she was the one who sought to find an inroad in his heart—*humans can't bear silence*. As she thought of Mercier's caution, she was surprised at how his words were beginning to have direct bearing on her life.

"Is Beam fine?"

"You could find out yourself," Edwin snapped. Mo's first thoughts were to draw herself to him, dismantle his defenses by offering sensuality. But she didn't feel up to rendering any pacifying service. What's more, she was not ready to dissipate his anger. It wasn't that she was unable to do so. The difficulty was her unwillingness to plumb the depths of another person's anger, much less such a person's individuality, never mind that her husband was the one in question.

"You're changing," Edwin said, minutes after he had spoken without a response from Mo.

"I know."

"What's happening?"

When he asked this, Mo saw that her husband's gaze was averted to the book.

"I don't know," she replied, closing the novel.

"But you know you're pulling inward too much?"

"Pulling inward" were words she had used to refer to him once, when they had been advised that it was best that she have few children, given the rupture of her uterus. Edwin spoke little in the subsequent days, keeping sleepless nights. She told him he was pulling inward and he smiled at her, a tired smile, but the morning after he became himself, asking for all the food he hadn't eaten. "Pulling inward" was, subsequently, accorded talisman status. Each partner was expected to smile, to "push outward" once the words had been spoken. But this time, it didn't work.

Mo did not see any reason to become herself again—not the self Edwin was used to. She doubted his ability to define her inwardness, or even his ability to understand Beam's screams. And she pitied the fact that he was standing in the terrain of illogic, sandwiched between Beam and herself.

"I don't think I want any children."

It came as a surprise even to her, that declaration. How long it had been within the unspeaking darkness of her mind, she couldn't tell. She did not look at Edwin when she said this.

Edwin chuckled and she closed her eyes. "That's an awful thing to say."

"I am afraid of being dependent."

"That's equally an awful thing to say."

She waited for him to speak again, still closing her eyes.

"You know what Beam said when she woke?" When she did not respond he said, "She said the same thing you're saying. That she didn't want to bother us with these dreams. I told her we were obliged to her, you have been with her all her life. And she said she didn't want that to continue, being the obligation of someone. Then I told her what I have told you—that it's an awful thing to say, even a disrespectful thing. But she didn't listen to me. She said what she wanted, instead, was to bear burdens, to fill her heart with concern for others."

Mo opened her eyes.

Edwin asked, "Is that what you want? To fill your heart with concern?"

"Beam is tired of being dependent. I have a different need; I am tired of carrying more than myself."

"That sounds nice," Edwin said, chuckling. But it was a light laugh; clearly he harbored some displeasure. Even in the chuckle Mo heard his chafing.

"And that's why you've stopped caring for your sister?"

It was a jab, an assault on her thoughts. She closed her eyes again, the only way she knew to respond to an unexpected affront. What was he thinking, she wondered, that had brought him to that conclusion? And was it true? She stood from the bed slowly, straightened her nightdress and said, "I'll go to the office. I need a quiet place."

Edwin said nothing. His silence hurt more than any word he could have said. He seemed to have said enough, all he needed to say anyway.

She parked in the Humanities parking lot and switched on the car's dome light. Then she grabbed Mercier's book from the passenger seat. She wanted to read it, but couldn't, thinking instead of Edwin's question. *And that's why you've stopped caring for your sister?*

How much could she care? Hadn't she cared enough? She closed her eyes, rubbed her face, knowing that if she sat any longer she could fall asleep.

In her office she switched on her computer and waited for it to boot. She thought of the words to write to Peter—they couldn't be about Mercier because she hadn't read him enough. They would be, she thought, about the overarching subject of leaving. Leaving meant more than a physical absence to her; it could be a mental reshaping, an overhaul of lifestyle, a drifting into singularity. All three options seemed to apply in her case.

When she wrote the first words of the email, she began to understand.

Dear Peter,

Do you ever feel like doing anything senseless only because it is senseless? Right now I feel that way. I want to leave this life behind.

Ask me, Peter, what is this life? There are no exact words, you know it.

I will seriously consider Bern. Given that, let me take the time to read Night Train. It seems to contain more than you have described. Only two sentences and I have taken grasp of senselessness. That means much to me, making a decision to leave my life as I know it because life is what we imagine we are living. It means that the right life to live is an imagined life.

I don't think Edwin or Beam can accord me an imagined life. Indeed Edwin has put the right logic in my head—I cannot carry anyone except myself, so I can't care for Beam anymore. Maybe I am cruel, but those dreams mean little to me. Perhaps if something tangible happens to Beam—an injury, a sickness—I could have reason to worry. Not when she's dreaming a senseless dream.

I will take Bern more seriously.

Moyosore

It was her grasp of senselessness that made Mo aloof to the changes around her, even on the campus. They were changes that could mean nothing to someone who was drifting to singularity, who contemplated the failures of leaving a life with others, for others, by others. And to complicate matters, since the night Edwin had accused her of caring less for Beam, she noticed that a collaborative energy pervaded her house—so forceful that she at once felt a pang of regret for inviting Beam to spend the months before her Youth Service at their home in Ife, rather than with their father in Badagry. Edwin and Beam spoke to each other while she was in their presence, with an audaciousness that inferred she was uninvited in their conversations. Usually she pretended to care, making eye contact with either of them while they conversed. But in truth she didn't; she was glad to be left out of the nuisance of daily life.

But one evening she overheard them speak about forthcoming protests, which Edwin predicted would be the biggest in a decade. How could she have missed that news? She rummaged through her mind and recalled seeing clusters of students, propaganda leaflets. She felt betrayed by her quest for singularity. She didn't regret her decision to "leave"; but it was like circling a boxing ring and not throwing a punch, seeing the need to leave without actually leaving.

That evening, a week after Beam's most recent dream, she asked her, "What's happening with the students?" Edwin looked at her without expression, his way of looking when he was irritated. She didn't mind. The night before they had had sex in a most difficult way, with their upper bodies covered; hers with a bandeau, his with a t-shirt. Increasingly she felt withdrawn from physical contact with him; two weeks earlier when she had began to speculate on individuality, it had only been her mind that sought change. Now, even her body seemed to be tired of the same man.

"They're protesting. The usual problems: light, water, reinstatement of expelled student activists, all that. But we hear the Vice Chancellor is calling in more policemen."

"Oh, okay. Sounds normal to me."

"It doesn't sound normal," Beam said. Edwin's head was now bowed and Mo could tell he was angry.

"Beam says she thinks this is the event that could make her dreams become real," Edwin said.

"That's ridiculous," Mo replied.

"Sister Moyo, let me explain it to you. You know me, you know me very well. This has not happened to me before, the same dreams for two weeks, five times in all. So when I heard this protest was going to happen, and I heard the scale it was going to take, I said, this is the revelation God has been giving to me, this is it—"

Mo didn't let her finish. "What have you done?"

"We're going to see the president of the Student Union tomorrow," Edwin said. Now it sounded to Mo like they were trying to win her favor.

"And you'll say what?" she said, hoping her sarcasm was evident.

"Tell him to call it off. It's that simple."

Mo shook her head. They waited for her to speak. There descended on them a silence she considered unforgiveable, seeing how much it stilled her thoughts, rendering her unaware. *Human beings can't bear silence.* She stood, walking away from her husband and younger sister, leaving them to their fantasies, their illogical dreams and conjoined futilities.

That evening, she wrote a one-line email to Peter:

One day, and I feel it's soon, I'll simply walk away.

Mo wouldn't know until the morning of the protests that the Student Union president had not listened to Edwin and Beam's irrationality. But Mo saw the failure in Beam's gaze, her muteness, as though she was listening for the sound of things to come. Mo was at the point where she felt no sense of responsibility—perhaps she'd brainwashed herself out of feeling any form of togetherness, preferring to think instead that in her world she coordinated every interaction, defined the limits of co-existence.

"You're fine?" she asked Beam, taking her seat, pulling open Mercier's book, not looking up at her sister. Beam said nothing in response. When Mo finally looked up, Beam was sobbing. Mo closed her eyes to think of a possible reaction.

"I'll call Daddy and tell him you're coming home." Her sister kept sobbing, saying nothing.

"You can't stay and keep making a mess of things, crying about a senseless dream. How can you invalidate a legitimate protest because of a meaningless dream? And you sit here crying like a baby for stupid reasons."

Her words bounced about in the room like a ball, as though each letter of each word was spoken distinctly, to establish the insult and admonish the addressee.

"Sister Moyo, if you want me to go," Beam said amid sobbing fits, "I will go right away."

"It's not just about leaving. You hear me? Let me ask you a question. If after the end of today's protest nothing happens, what will you do?"

Mo had asked rhetorically, but Beam answered with an inverse question. "And if something happens, what do you think I will do?"

Mo watched her sister angrily, thinking of the time when they were younger and she could hit her with justification. But Beam was twenty-three-years old, equally an adult, capable of intending the consequences of her actions and inactions.

"I don't care what you do if something happens," Mo told her. "I don't care what you do with your life. Just get out of my way."

Beam resumed her sobbing; Mo turned to a fresh page of Mercier's book.

II

You set up a fence in your head, and that is the pen you want for your life, expecting the perimeter to encase the lives of everyone you love. But you find the fence becomes constricting, that there are certain persons who wish to leave your enclosure. In my case, it was my wife; her departure was like forcefully breaking away from my prison.

Everything happened at once. The events succeeding the protests created what I considered an infinitely tethered moment, the end of everything as I had known it. I felt shame as things unfolded because, although I had perceived a looming catastrophe, I hadn't imagined the extent of possible damage, the legion of demons that wished to leap into view.

That afternoon I announced to my wife and her sister that a student had died, hit by a stray bullet. In the hurried way I announced the mishap, I didn't notice the postures of Mo and her sister. While Mo's head was bent as though it was inscribed in the book she was reading—a book I once thought I should shred into pieces—Beam's eyes were closed, her forehead creased. When I mentioned the bullet and the death, my eyes were on Beam, not because I recalled her dreams, but simply because Mo hadn't been much of a partner in the previous weeks. The truth was that while I showed concern for Beam's dreams, I more or less played a perfunctory role, seeing how distanced Mo had become, how self-seeking. Mo said nothing, even when I turned to her. By this time Beam was walking out of the living room. I saw that Mo didn't look disturbed by the news; if anything, the expression on her face was one of deliberate nonchalance. I wasn't interested in making an argument, since she increasingly irritated me. My thought as I sat opposite her was that Mo and I weren't perfectly compatible any longer. For one, I didn't believe in the imaginary as she did; there were times she compared a real-life action with a happening in a novel. And times when she saw no point in religious duty, saying if God was as almighty as we claimed, there was no point in service, in spending our lives being obliged to him.

Beam's groans took us unaware. They were not like her usual dream-screams, which were fringed with unbelievability. Her voice that late afternoon, which came to us from her room, sounded like the definition of pain. I stood before Mo did, not turning to look at her, only seeing her stirring frame from the corner of my eye. I took unsteady steps, sensing danger, a certain sense of finality. Perhaps Beam's groans were what it all came to, the preceding weeks of dream-screaming becoming insolent precursors.

There, on her bedroom floor, she held a cooking knife that was wedged in her stomach. She was groaning in pain. I ran to her side, staining my hazel colored pants in the process. I heard Mo's voice. She said, "Shit," repeatedly. "My God!" I yelled. Beam was making unintelligent sounds, seeming to affirm that in the first place all of this was unintelligent, illogical—for why would she wish to take her life?

"This is what you want to do, eh? Kill yourself?" Mo said, as I tried to lift Beam out of the room. Mo was standing by the door. When I succeeded in lifting Beam, Mo was still by the door, now hysterical in her affront. "This is foolish! You want to kill yourself because of your stupid dream? Oh shit! Shit, shit, shit!" When I was out of the house, there was no one to help open the car. Mo hadn't come out. I screamed our neighbor's name and his wife came out, shouted, and I told her my keys were in my pocket. All we did was shout. Even Mo's affronts, as she still stood in Beam's room, were shouts. Although she hollered more "Shit!" than anything else.

And Mo did not come to the hospital with us. It was my neighbor's wife who sat in the back with Beam. She was screaming, "Oh Jesus, have mercy on us, this girl will not die. Oh Jesus."

While driving I kept thinking, "Oh Jesus."

III

She packed her things and left. I didn't—couldn't—understand. It was as though I was being assaulted with unreasonableness. Why did Beam try to kill herself? For what reasons had Mo left?

When Beam was successfully admitted into the hospital, the knife removed, surgery done, a blood transfusion completed, I returned to meet my wife's absence. Some of her things remained—her shoes, some clothes, most of her jewelry. But there were no books. She had taken all the books in the glass shelf away, except the Bibles. When I saw that the books in her bedside cabinet were gone as well, I suspected she wouldn't return.

Could there be words to explain how I felt—like I had been beaten with a club and was in pain but not bleeding? Like I was in a trancelike reality? There could be no way, I tell you, to negotiate the suddenness of her leaving, of being caught off guard.

Her note was only two lines long.

Edwin, I am out. Do not bother, I will be fine, as I trust you will be too. Take Abimbola to my father. I told him she was returning. —Moyo

How does one read such a note? I shredded it as soon as I was sure I had memorized the message. I walked to the living room thirsty for meaning. While I walked pieces of Mo's note fell to the floor so that, by the time I pulled open the refrigerator door, the litter formed a trail to the bedroom.

While I drank water I remembered a French phrase Mo had used in one of our conversations in the days when she listened for my criticism as she reveled in the imaginative, polishing her critical essays about the intricate lives of characters in African-American novels. *Espirit d'escalier*, a French phrase for when you realize that perfect verbal comeback but are too late to deploy it. That was the way I felt, as though I should have said something a long time ago. But how does one know when to speak, and when not to? And how could I have measured the rightness of time between speaking, waiting to speak, and saying what needed to be said, words that dispelled unreasonableness?

I did as she told me, taking Beam to their father, averting his gaze, avoiding his questions, and leaving Badagry the same day.

IV

The happenings at church spurred me to start writing imaginary letters to Mo. I missed her prejudices, her spiritual nonchalance, our oppositeness. On the Sunday after her departure I lied each time I was asked of her whereabouts. "She traveled for a conference," I said to the first inquirer, and, "She had to see her father,"

I said to another. Two others asked, and I evenly distributed the lies. So, after the first Sunday of her absence, I wrote a letter, taking a sheet from the drawer in our wardrobe. She must have taken the one for her departure note from the same place. I didn't notice that there were already existing words on the page.

It was Mo's handwriting, the way she wrote when in a hurry. Had she intended for me to see that?

The day that ended with everything different in the life of Raimund Gregorius began like countless other days.

What could she have been thinking? Could she have been alluding to the day that ended with everything different in our lives—Beam's attempted suicide, her departure? I became certain that it was from the book she had been reading before her disappearance.

I had once stolen a glance at the book's blurb while she slept. While looking at the book I had had the feeling of imprudence: that if I was not conscientious enough, the knowledge she obtained from the book would make her transcendental, and I would not be able to look at her without deference. I had looked at the blurb of the book long enough to to get the gist: One day a teacher named Raimund Gregorius suddenly quits his ordinary life, and for no apparent reason sets off on a journey across Europe.

Was this what she had done? Acted without any apparent reason? Hadn't she accused Beam and I of the same disease of illogicality?

Yet, despite the senselessness of it all, I wanted her back. There was no way it was going to happen, seeing as she hadn't disclosed her whereabouts. So I wrote imaginary letters, or notes. I was bad at telling stories, given that I thought narratives were unreachable, things above our heads. And so the only story I could tell was the drama that had played out in church. I even dared to believe that if I described the events well enough I could draw Mo into spiritual responsibility, make her the Christian I wished she could be. Not that the church story was particularly inspiring.

I wrote the short letter in one sitting, hardly lifting my head. I sat on the bed, placing the same sheet that Mo had used for her hurriedly-written note on the nightstand, and began to write:

Today at church there was mild fracas when Seeds, the Youth publication, was distributed. It was spearheaded by Dr. Addo—you know how he acts. He walked about the church shouting "Justice Ike, come here!" threatening to terminate the boy's studentship if he didn't apologize in open for the essay. So, naturally, I was inclined to read the publication, to know for myself. His essay, "Transcending Normality," questioned the usualness of the choir's songs, the archaic disposition of the choirmaster, and the trendiness of youth. If I remember correctly, he ended with "Change is at our heels." And I wondered, what is change? I, too, have a penchant for normalcy.

If you return we could debate this, I'm sure.

When I stood up I felt numb in my legs, but thought that the numbness was not just my legs; it extended everywhere. I closed my eyes, feeling tears in them. I had never imagined Mo's disappearance.

The following Sunday I wrote another imaginary letter to Mo. I used the same sheet I'd written the first letter on. I anticipated the numbness of my legs after writing, yet I was eager to speculate on how the events in church had raised the same questions that bedeviled my relationship with Mo.

This time, Moyo, it's an open disagreement between the Choirmaster and his assistant. The church service had ended and various

157

units were meeting, mostly to discuss the forthcoming retreat. Adjacent to where the ushers met was the choir. I can't tell who spoke first, but the first loud voice was the Choirmaster's. "You are too ambitious, Lekan. I know what you want. I know you want my position." The church hall quieted, everyone became attuned to the Choirmaster's raised voice. Mr. Lekan spoke next, sounding like he was in complete mastery of his inflections. And there was certainly a tinge of mischief and calculated arrogance in his voice. "I am only saying that we should have an election. If we are content with our present Choirmaster, he will be re-elected. It is dangerous to assume we want him to remain, and it is equally dangerous to assume we want him to leave. So, the simple thing to do is to have an election and see how things turn out."

I didn't, I couldn't, keep listening. Right there in the chaos, I paused to listen to your voice, the one I now imagine. You would have, in your heady manner, argued about the complexity of church life. How did democratic ideals fit into theocratic ones? How could there be a government of an elected representative under an unelected, sovereign God? You see, you'd have said, church life is void of reason.

And I wouldn't have understood why the next Sunday you'd still come with me to church, sit in the corner where you usually sat, writing poems on the Sunday bulletin, poems you never considered witty enough.

And that's why I want you back.

The Friday following my second letter, I attended the church vigil, which was held every last Friday of the month. I attended because I had recently become an insomniac, sleeping very little, awakened by even the slightest noise. Sometimes when I awoke, the first thing I thought of was Beam's dreams: Why hadn't I begun to have such dreams? Perhaps our problem with the logicality of the dream is its peculiarity; perhaps if everyone had dreams that had profound evidence in reality, we could have been proactive in seeking to prevent the death of the student. Yet I wasn't willing to engage much with things I could not understand—I had never fancied philosophy as a means to approach life's complexity. And I had never wanted to engage with the intangible, the unknown parameters of existence.

At the church vigil I saw the Choirmaster only once. He was sitting in one of the back pews, his head raised in a manner that showed he was listening disinterestedly to the things being said. I didn't know when he left, but I turned during a prayer session and saw he was no longer there. About ten minutes after I noticed his absence, the Assistant Chaplain tapped my shoulder and said, "Come quickly, Sir." I walked with him to the back of the church. "There's been an incident," he said. "The Choirmaster called the Chaplain and said he was attacked by hoodlums." I frowned, flummoxed. "He's still lying in his car; I can't tell what state he's in."

"Where was he attacked?" I asked.

"In the theatre car park. Just a few minutes ago. He called."

"He called on phone?"

"Yes. We have to go to him now. You're the only usher here tonight, so I came to you."

"Let's go."

A few hours later in my house, I took a clean sheet of paper, placed it on the coffee table, and kneeled to write a final letter to Mo. This time it wasn't imaginary. The attack on the Choirmaster had changed things—such a tangential event, yet it had introduced a new mode to my quest for Mo's return.

Who would've believed, Mo, that the Choirmaster could be attacked on campus? Such a quiet, easy-going man? Such a strange thing to happen in a campus that has few security problems. You know how it's said that after a student was hacked to death by cultists in '99 and students rose in one accord to—permit this word—exorcise cultists and since they succeeded, the campus has become relatively safe. So how do we explain that, at the theatre car park, just as he was coming out of his car, sticks and blows and hits descended on the Choirmaster, injuring him?

When we got to him, the doors of his car were open, and he was lying in the backseat, groaning. We took him to my car, and while we drove to the health center, he said to us, "I was going to send an email in my office, would someone help me send it? Today's the deadline." I asked him, "What email sir?" He had difficulty speaking, but he managed to mutter his address and password, and that it was an acceptance to an invitation to a conference in Kaduna.

When I was sending his email, I wondered about the complexity of leading a group, being situated within a collective order. You have done well to let me know why you left; you didn't want to be in a collective anymore, you wanted to opt for individuality.

Doesn't memory mean anything to you, Mo? Is there no sufficient memorial of our marriage that could enable you believe in the workability of our togetherness? Are you blind to the impossibility of singularity in this world, the irrefutable fact of co-existence? It's not, as you think, only about having children, or taking care of Beam. Togetherness is more than people, or living with people.

The day you find that out, you will return.

And I will be waiting.

After signing out of the Choirmaster's email, I signed into mine and found Mo's email. It was a thread of exchanges between her and a certain Peter, a correspondence that began weeks before her disappearance. Why had she forwarded the thread to me?

Her explanation was, "I've been thinking of how angry you might feel. Perhaps these emails will help you understand."

I became angry. It was the first time I was angry at her irrationality. I was angry especially because, even after reading the emails, I didn't understand why she forwarded them to me.

Was it a good sign? Could she be having doubts about her newfound individuality?

That was when I decided to write a final letter and send it to her by email. I hadn't wished to send any of the letters I wrote, so the question of sending them by email hadn't arisen. My letters were, first and foremost, letters of questioning, speculation, never of irritation or exasperation, more or less an inward groping for Mo's return. Yet despite her craving for individuality, her war against ordinariness, she had written to me first. It seemed to be an opportunity. I felt inspired to type out all the imaginary letters I had written and send them to her by email.

That was what I did.

The Sunday following the attack on the Choirmaster, the Chaplain led a prayer session for his recovery. My eyes were fixed on the choir, especially on the area in which Mr. Lekan sat, I saw that his head was bowed, a book open in front of him from which he seemed to be reading while the prayers were recited. He reminded me of Mo on that afternoon when I'd announced the death of the student, the realization of Beam's dream.

Six

MONKEY'S WEDDING

I

He said he liked being wet, enjoyed the immense satisfaction he got when he was drenched to the skin, his shirt gummed to his body and his face dripping. He said he wished the car were roof-less, so that as the rain fell we would understand what it meant to be wet, to take in rain without restraint. I was not sure he was talking to me. I was sitting closest to him, so I guessed he was. But I said nothing. And he became silent, not speaking about the rain again until we were close to Ife. Eventually the rain stopped and the early evening seemed clear and still. This time, when he spoke, he turned to me. He was sitting by the window. "You know, my sister, this life is funny. See how the rain was here some minutes ago and in another minute it is gone."

I responded, "My name is not Sister." He chuckled, and said nothing to me again. I told the driver I would alight at the campus gate. When the driver stopped for me to get out, I saw that the man stirred too. After the van sped off, he was standing beside me, as though he had been there with me all my life. We were standing across the road from the gate, so we had to cross over. When the road was clear, he held my hand, looked ahead, and led me to the other side. I could have protested. Yet, as when he had stood beside me, it seemed perfectly normal.

When we walked the short distance to the campus gate, he told me, "Someone is coming for me. You can join us." Up until then, I hadn't looked at his face, hadn't taken a close look. I examined him as we waited for his car. His face was like an unfinished painting in which all colors except one were present. I do not think he was handsome, but he possessed something that demanded attention.

"Why are you looking at me like that?" he asked me.

I could have told a lie. Yet the words that came to my head were the truth. "I have not looked at you closely."

He smiled. I noticed that he was not regarding me while he talked, and I figured he might not have looked at me, at least not in the way I had observed. "Why do you need to look at me, sister?"

While I contemplated my response, a van pulled up beside us.

He smiled to the driver, who smiled in return, and I forgot that I had wanted to respond, to chastise him for calling me sister again. He opened the van's passenger door and motioned for me to enter. I did, and then he joined me. I noticed that the driver, who had turned to face us as we made ourselves comfortable, was smiling. I tried to figure out whether his smile was genuine; I wasn't sure.

The man made no conversation with me while we were in the van; he had only given a response to the driver when he was asked about his journey. When we were at the bus stop, he asked me where I was going. "Staff Quarters. Road 18," I told him, and he nodded. Prior to then I thought that he was really cheerful, and that all the talk he had made with me in the van was to flirt with me. But when he asked me where I was headed, and I saw in his eyes the lack of glee, I began to wonder whether he was really interested in flirting — or whether there was something else that perturbed him. And since I figured that he wasn't interested in me in the way I had first thought, I asked him, "Your name?" He replied, "Chika." I was sure he would ask for mine, but he didn't, and I felt lame, stupid even.

Because we had to get to the Conference Center, he told the driver to let him off there. The driver drove into the parking lot, and when he exited, he told me, "Sister, I would like to call you sometime." I knew what he was asking. I could have declined, given how discourteous he was being by leaving me alone with the driver. Nonetheless, I acquiesced. I dictated the number to him. "I will call you sometime," he said, and I nodded. The driver moved the vehicle and I fixed my eyes on the steering wheel, so that I would not be tempted to look at his retreating figure, so that I would not see the something that demanded attention.

I thanked the driver and asked him to thank Chika on my behalf. My mother welcomed me at the door and asked how my trip had been. Then she asked who had been in the vehicle, why a Conference Center van had come to drop me off. I told her I had met Chika, without mentioning his name, and she looked at me and smiled in a way that reminded me that the week before she had asked what my plans were for settling down, if there was anyone I was seeing. Such topics formed a brick wall between us; on one side she was pushing for information, on the other side I was withholding. I went into the house and sat in a chair. My mother was watching a movie on Africa Magic, a channel I detested. I could have made the case for indigenous movie making, how it was important we patronized Nollywood as much as, or more than, Hollywood. But there was no reason to make the argument with myself; I wasn't a stakeholder anyway.

Between watching the movie and shouting orders to Salatau, who lived with us and cooked our meals and washed my father's underwear, my mother asked me if I was choosing Ife or Ibadan. I told her I wasn't sure. I had been offered admission to study for my Masters at either Ife or the University of Ibadan. My mother nodded when I said I wasn't sure, but I felt she was dissenting; I

165

felt she was advising me to get out already, that at twenty-four I was old enough to own a home and manage it, like other women my age.

"Where's Daddy?" I asked her.

"Meeting," she replied, her eyes still glued to Africa Magic. I looked up at the television and saw that there was a man atop a woman, jerking, simulating sex. My mother sighed and averted her eyes.

I smiled to myself, thinking of how sex suddenly became immoral and detestable when it was in the public domain.

II

Chika called me two days after we had met and I responded with nonchalance. I had thought little of him after we parted ways, but there were fleeting moments I remembered his face and the fact that he had called me Sister.

"Oh, it's you," I said, when I heard his voice. He said, "Yes. Sure. How are you?"

"Great. I'm fine."

The conversation went on like that, each of us indulging the other, going roundabout. I began to wonder why he had called, and was a few seconds away from asking him directly when he said, "I was thinking we could see each other again. I wasn't really myself that day, you know."

"Okay." And I immediately became sorry that I was indulging him too much, that he was really flirting with me.

"So, how do we see each other?"

I paused a while, waiting for some click in my head, a confirmation that I was doing the right thing if I responded positively. There was none. He asked me, "You don't want us to meet? I can come to your house if you don't want to come out."

I wasn't really shocked that he said this. From the conversation's outset there was a measure of determination in his voice, an assuredness that made him sound different from other men that patronized me. For a second I began to wonder if the female life wouldn't be summed, at the close of human existence, as a life of male patronage. "So you can come to my house if I don't want to come out?"

I heard him chuckle. "Yes. No. Well, I'm not sure. I have to hope otherwise."

This time I chuckled. I asked him if he had some place in mind. He said it would be fine if we chose the Conference Center to avoid any inconvenience, since I lived nearby. After I agreed, he said, "Is five o'clock okay?"

It was Friday; ordinarily I would have gone for choir rehearsal at church. "Yes. I'll come."

I heard him sigh, and I realized that he could have been nervous, which seemed improper in the circumstances, in the larger scheme of things where women were meant to be patronized by men.

I remembered my last boyfriend, Mark, who started smoking the week after I said yes to him. When I asked him about it he said every man picked up a habit when he met a woman, if he loved her dearly. That was four years ago, in my third year in college. Despite being uncertain about how things would turn out between Chika and me, I assumed he too would pick up a habit.

He took me to his office first; it seemed spacious, the kind of office that belonged to the manager of a warehouse. I was surprised I had not guessed earlier that he was the manager of the Conference Center, and felt slightly annoyed that he had not told me. Yet, I could not confront him with my surprise or anger, seeing that he was in good spirits. He opened a small refrigerator that stood beside his chair, and pulled out a can of beer. I told him I didn't drink alcohol, no matter how little. He looked down, clearly disappointed, perhaps with himself, and said, "I drink only beer."

I could tell he wasn't lying. And I could tell that he thought I thought he was lying. "I believe you."

He nodded when I said that, opened the refrigerator again and this time pulled out a bottle of water. "I could have taken you to the restaurant, but I'm not sure you'll like the food. The women on duty today are the worst set."

I smiled. "So you group them like that: good better best?"

He smiled too. "As a matter of fact, yes. We don't do too well on Fridays. Maybe it is moral to do that."

Our talk didn't seem to be heading in any direction. We hadn't gotten to the point where we could talk intimately, trade our lives. I sensed he was not ready for that. More importantly, I sensed he wasn't sure what he wanted with me, from me, and what words we could use to define our friendship, if we became friends.

"Let's go to the restaurant," I told him.

"Are you sure? The food is not too good." He was looking at me intently when he said this, and I figured he was really concerned for me.

"I'm sure," I said.

When we got to the restaurant he asked me what I wanted. Before then he had beckoned to one of the waitresses, who had been sitting watching Africa Magic when we entered, and asked for the menu. Although there was a copy of the menu on each table in the restaurant, I knew that the waitress would offer a better one, orally, as though the written one was a camouflage to convey the sense of a good restaurant. The waitress told us there was rice and pounded yam, egusi soup. She spoke without caution; I felt she should have cared that she was talking with her manager and his guest. So I knew I had the option of rice or pounded yam. I told him rice, which in turn he told the waitress, who had too much makeup on—she seemed too dressed up for her job. Wearing a blue cotton gown, her uniform, made her look unconventional.

Chika asked me, when the waitress had gone, "Are you sure you want to eat?"

I told him I was sure. "You're being too careful."

When the waitress came with my food, he told her to bring another plate, for him, a bottle of Guinness, and I saw that she looked disturbed, as though she had been called to do something her job did not dictate.

"Would you wait for me or you'll start eating?"

I told him I would wait. He pulled the plate toward himself. I told him, "You're being too careful."

He shook his head and said with a straight face, "I shouldn't be?"

I smiled and told him, "I don't know if you should be, or why you should be."

He shook his head again and looked at the door where a man had called out to him, asking something about the bus. Chika replied by only saying okay, and looked back at me. I saw that the man hesitated before retreating, then I looked back at Chika. His eyes seemed tired. The waitress returned with another plate, without the Guinness, and Chika looked at her, shook his head, and asked her if there was some place she should work other than the Conference Center.

"I am sorry, Sir," she said, in a way that showed that his question suggested negation, the end of employment.

When she was off again, he looked at me and said, "I bore people easily. Right now, I don't know what to say."

It shocked me that he was lowering my expectations—each time I wanted to believe he was interested in romance, in flirting, he said something that floored me, and made me curious. "How old are you?" I asked.

My intention was to mock him after his response, call him a baby for having no words, but then I realized it was probably an inordinate reason, and I was incorrectly plotting the graph of our conversation. The waitress brought the Guinness. He opened it immediately. I was grateful for the pause, which made my question linger, and I felt it circled over us. I started to eat, only because I wanted to allay his concerns about the food. It had too much salt, little pepper, and I imagined how I could have easily done better.

We ate in silence, sharing no words until he was halfway done. He pushed his plate aside and gulped the rest of his beer. By this time I had eaten only a quarter of my food. "You don't need to finish it, really."

I pushed it aside, as he had done, and I felt annoyed that he was being too considerate. It made it seem as though he considered me too weak to eat bad food. "You should sack the kitchen staff," I said, hoping my irritation was apparent enough.

"It is not as simple as you think. There is a long chain of administrative bureaucracy. I can only recommend stuff."

I nodded and said, "You have not told me your age."

He said, "Ah. I'm thirty-eight."

"You're fourteen years my senior. I don't know if you look older or younger."

"Is that really important? Whether I look older or younger?"

"Well, I guess so. I'm not sure."

"If I was younger, I might live longer."

"What?"

"When the rain starts, it has a longer time to fall. As it progresses, its time shortens."

"You like the rain."

"It's always a good model."

"I see."

When we stood, he thanked me for coming to see him, and said he would call me, to see if I would oblige him again. I thought of his words, living longer if he was younger, and it confused me. I could have asked him. But he suddenly became dismissive, restless even, and I thought I caught him sniffing, stopping himself from shedding a tear. He said he would take me home in his car. I nodded because I wanted to please him somewhat, to indulge him now that I felt he was distressed.

While he drove he said he was going to explore the small details of the university. I asked him how he intended to do that and he spoke of how, for example, he intended to find out which architect designed the Conference Center, why there was some part of the building still incomplete, and whether it was right to have meetings of the Governing Council of the University in the Seminar Room. The details he sought to know sounded extraneous, but I couldn't mention their irrelevancy, as I couldn't mention how befuddled I was at who he was, what was going on in his life. After he spoke about the details he intended to uncover, he became silent, kept his eyes steady, and although I tried to find meaning in his eyes, I didn't. I could only see his receding hairline, which suggested he would be bald in another five years or so. He drove quite slowly, and I anticipated that he would try to make conversation with me. He didn't. He kept his eyes steady, his hands on the wheel.

When we arrived at Road 18, he asked for my house number. For the first time I saw that all the houses on the road looked similar, and that despite the individuality we tried to express, something as simple as the pattern of our houses could make us a collective. "The last house, down the road," I told him.

171

He spoke in hushed tones, as though he was speaking blasphemy. "Okay. Tell me when we get there." We got to my house and I saw that my father's car was there; he was in. When I was younger, some two years before then, I wouldn't have had the guts to allow a man to bring me home in his car. But since I had graduated from the university, I took the liberty to be freer, and my father, surprisingly, hadn't complained. He stopped the car, pulled the handbrake, and said, "I am sorry if I behaved strangely."

I was surprised he knew, which meant there was a time when he wouldn't have behaved the way he had, that he was comparing today with other days. "Are you okay?" I asked.

"Okay? Really, I don't know what that means." He wasn't looking at me, his eyes were still steady.

I stopped myself from opening the car door and walking out. There was something that I didn't understand then, that kept me there. Considering how new our relationship was—or whatever it was we had—I was surprised. "You're not okay then. You want to tell me what it is?"

He turned to me, looking at my face briefly. "Ah, Sister, I don't think you would understand. Really." I guess he saw how let down those words made me feel, and that I wasn't sure whether it was his calling me sister or saying I wouldn't understand that made me feel aggrieved.

He said, "I am sorry. It is just that things are more complex than I imagined they would be. I thought you could help me out. When I saw you, I said here's a beautiful lady; she would take this thing away. But you are more than that. You don't remind me of beauty. You remind me of…erm…life."

When he was done, I looked toward my house and saw that the curtains were drawn, and someone was peering out from behind them. "Okay then," I said.

He had resumed looking steadily ahead of him, holding the steering wheel. Even before I closed the door he had started the car. When I closed the door, he honked and drove off.

That night I found it difficult to sleep. The mystery of Chika kept my mind busy. I thought adding notes to my digital diary—my private Twitter account—would exorcise some of my unfounded anxiety. I kept my account private—I wanted to see how the discipline and economy of the form could help me understand. In tweeting I found expression for the things circling in my head. But then I just stared at my phone, reading and re-reading previous entries as if I could find a clue in the narrative of my subconscious. I couldn't.

III

I met an old man—he was called Papa by all the staff of the Olufe Old Peoples' Home. At the gate of the Home there was a verse from the Bible, half-quoted, "He has put eternity in their hearts." It made me wonder, as we five members of the Chapel's Welfare Committee and I entered, if life held any paraphernalia aside from the promise of death. It was a Saturday. Earlier, we had agreed to visit the Home, to reach out to its residents and speak to them about Jesus and extend the benevolent arm of the Chapel.

The Home was owned and managed by the wife of a professor of physics; they were also members of the church. Only the silence ringing through the Home seemed out of place—not the bright red chaise lounges in the large sitting room, nor the Persian rug, not even the wall-size banner that pictured smiling old people and the name of the Home; no, not even the clock wearied by age and a lifetime of chiming. We sat, waiting for the proprietress. She arrived smiling the practiced smile of a hostess and told us it was best to divide the provisions we brought between us—that we'd be assigned to individual residents.

173

I was assigned to Papa.

He seemed an agile man, alert and talkative. He smiled the same sort of smile of the proprietress. I sat on the only chair in the room. There was a bed, a TV, a shelf above the television, and a small refrigerator. The room was quaint but seeing as there were few possessions and furniture, it looked spacious enough. Papa was lanky and I guessed that in his youth he must have been athletic.

He spoke first. "Everyone comes here as if we're beggars." That seemed like a blow. And he'd said it smiling. "People think because we're not in our own homes, that we're in need of pity. I don't want any person's pity. I have enough for myself already."

"I'm here to keep you company." I knew it was a stupid thing to say. I waited for his response, another blow.

But he said instead, "Well, that's a new one. No one has said that before."

I regained my nerve. "You get a lot of visitors?"

"A handful." I saw that his hands were shaking. He reached for the refrigerator and pulled out a bottle of gin. "It's what keeps me alert. I've been drinking for as long as I can remember. And I can't remember being drunk."

"They allow you to drink, here?"

He chuckled, took a swig, capped the bottle, and returned it to the refrigerator. "My son pays for this place, this room. It's not just a Christian charity. It's a business."

I nodded.

"You're a beautiful lady," he said.

I looked down, pulling closer the bag that contained his share of the provisions we'd brought. "This is for you, Sir," I said.

"They call me Papa."

"Okay." We were silent for a while. I didn't like the fact that he complimented me on my beauty, or the fact that up till then I hadn't said anything about Christ, and yet we were on an evangelical campaign. I looked at his hands, they still shook. He seemed to be at least seventy; he had the kind of face that was old but ageless.

"You know, when I saw you, I thought of a certain woman I had known. We worked together. A long time ago. She spoke little, only spoke of work, and I wanted to marry her. But she never wanted to get married."

I wanted to say something, so that his words, his recollection of a time past, would not pointlessly fall to the ground. But I became confused as to why he was telling me about a colleague he wanted to marry; it sounded as though he said that to every visitor.

"What's your name?"

"Mosun."

"Mosun. Is that a complete name?"

"It's Mosunmola."

"If you come back again I will tell you about my life."

Someone knocked; it was time to go. I nodded toward him. I didn't promise to return.

IV

Chika did not call me. A week after we had last seen each other I went to his office. When he opened the door I kept my eyes down, fixed on the carpet, so that our eyes would not meet. But it was impossible to keep my eyes fixed on his floor because his cologne hit my nose sharply; I looked up at him. He was smiling, and I couldn't help but smile back, despite thinking that I was being too cheap, giving myself up to his grasp too easily, letting him hold the part of myself that was most vital. "Come in," he said. And he waited for me to sit before he sat and said, "I guessed you'd come. I couldn't bear to call you again after I treated you like that.

I said foolish things to you." The air conditioner in his office blew so strongly it caused me to sneezed.

"You want me to turn it off?" he asked.

I said, "In a minute." I waited for him to speak next, but he was waiting for me to speak again. So I said, "You did not sound foolish the last time. You are keeping something from me."

He chuckled. Looking at his face I remembered thinking once that it looked like an incomplete painting. Now his eyes seemed dimmer, drawn with bags underneath them, which might have come from crying too much or sleeping too few hours, or both. "That's very interesting, Sister. You think I am keeping something from you?"

By the way he looked at me I figured he knew that I knew he was being evasive. I said nothing.

Then he told me. "You are right. I am keeping something from you. It is not a question of whether you deserve to be told. It is just...erm...I am not ready to speak about it now." There we were, speaking about what was ongoing in his life as though we were childhood friends, as though we hadn't only just met, as though we had the right to ourselves. "I'd like you to listen to a song. From *Cadillac Records*."

I asked what Cadillac Records was.

"A movie," he said. "They tried to chronicle the advent of the blues." He played a song from his phone titled "Forty Days and Forty Nights." It was the story of a man whose lady had been absent for that amount of time. I saw that he was disappointed with the way I received the song.

"What do you want from me?" I asked him. I surprised myself, and I tried to imagine what effect the question would have on him. He did not seem surprised; it looked as if he had asked himself the same thing. He sat up on his chair and leaned closer to me. I asked him again, "What do you want from me, Chika?"

"I heard you the first time."

"So?"

"You're too demanding."

"I'm what?"

"Too demanding."

"For asking what you want from me? For wanting to know what is wrong with you?"

"You are asking too much from me. I want to take it slowly. I am not prepared for this much."

"This is serious, and maybe stupid."

"All right. I'm sick."

"I don't care anymore. I don't want to know."

I stood up and left, thinking that if I had weighed things carefully I would have stayed. But I was angry that I had let too much out of myself, and that I couldn't explain why we were at loggerheads at only our third meeting.

V

Perhaps it was my anger that made me remember Papa. Or perhaps it was because I felt he would take all of me if I gave him enough attention. I went to see him.

He didn't smile when he saw me. "I knew you'd come back." That moment I regretted coming, detested his arrogance, tagged him a haughty septuagenarian in my mind. He saw I was annoyed at his greeting. His smile was a flash of lightning.

"Well, I am here," I said.

"You brought anything for me? The food they give here is crap."

"You told me to come and listen."

He seemed disappointed; I felt foolish. It hadn't made sense coming. "I'm too tired to talk. I was awake all night."

"What were you doing?"

"Reading."

"Reading," I repeated.

"I asked them to get me every Mia Couto in the bookshop. They got me two. I read both through the night."

He pointed at two slim books atop the refrigerator: *Voices Made Night* and *Every Man Is a Race*. I turned toward him; his eyes were fixed on me.

"I've been thinking about my son."

"Your son?"

"Oh yes. He brought me here. I was demanding too much, he said. I used to live with him, and I wonder how we managed to live together those months. Three months."

"You don't have a good relationship with him?"

He sighed and smiled his flashy-brief smile. "He hates me." In one instant his demeanor calcified—he became a needy old man, one devoid of bliss, one to whom life had been unflinchingly cruel.

"Hate is a very strong word," I said. Yet, quite tangentially, at that moment I felt how much I was a stranger to myself, having no clue as to why, despite the pain in his eyes, I responded without compassion, only commenting on the word he'd used.

"He hates me, I'm sure. He has never come here, always sending someone."

The silence seemed infinite. I thought of how I'd failed as a Christian. And I felt worse knowing that I was thinking of myself, not Papa. It was Papa's mild chuckle that broke the silence.

"'Women are an endless territory, and when we journey through them, we always get lost.' That's Mia Couto, and I know it probably sounds chauvinist, and you're a woman. But that's, in short, the story of my life."

"A woman is the story of your life?"

178

"Well, if my son is my life, his mother is my story."

"I don't understand that."

He laughed, then frowned. I couldn't fathom how he did it—switching between expressions of pain and painlessness. It wasn't an act I had mastered, or could master.

"You know I didn't sleep well..." he muttered.

I stood. His eyes were still closed.

When I was at the door I heard his voice. "You shouldn't be angry with me. I just fell out of mood today. I'd like to talk about my son, someday. If you come back."

"Bye, Papa," was all I said.

On the bus ride home my mind was a tangle of thoughts. I couldn't make sense of the past couple of weeks. Finding no resolution I recorded the moment in my Twitter diary: *The two men in my life are total strangers. They're making me a stranger to myself.* And: *Clarity can't be far away.*

VI

Two days later Chika contacted me to apologize for our last meeting. I was in my father's study reading *The Essence of Man in Community*. I was preparing to get a Master's in sociology. There were times I had doubts about it though; perhaps I should have pursued a career in psychology, to better understand human interactions. There was something about the study of community that trivialized individuality.

My phone beeped and it was Chika, a text message. "I am sorry for last time. Really." I read it over and over.

My phone had a large screen, so his text occupied a single line. All those feelings, all the anger I felt when I remembered our last conversation, was summarized in a single line. I wanted to reply to him, something nasty, call his bluff, but I lacked the guts to do so. And I began to think it was me that actually wanted something from him. I checked my head for an answer, anything from our three meetings that could validate my assumption. I couldn't find a pointer, a clue.

I knew I could find the opening if I pushed on long enough. I had found something of its nature once, after my stint with Babatunde. At that time, I could feel a hole in me, some weightless but deep matter that occupied the space that was my heart. I didn't doubt the possibility of having the hole; I walked around campus, going on errands for my parents, waiting to be posted for my compulsory service year. I would stop at a shop with a mirror and look at my chest area, examining it for a possible opening, as one checks to see if the pus in a boil has seeped out. This wasn't an illusion for me—I knew my life had come to the point where love had to be meaningful, when I should find a man and he could look at me and be frank with me and see the hole in my heart. Babatunde's exit had made me conscious of that need, and I remember feeling grateful. Then I went for my service year and I lost the feeling of a hole in the space that was my heart. Later I remembered the feeling, I laughed at myself. But now, remembering it again, I found I could not laugh at the weirdness of it. I had lied to myself when I had mocked myself. Now the emptiness became truer, as though reality had swollen beyond measure, as though Chika's entry had everything to do with the sudden re-realization.

He came to my house; it was the day after his text message. My sister opened the door. I was sitting with my mother in the living room. She had, for some astonishing reason, chosen to watch CNN, listening intently to the analysis that followed a volcanic eruption in Iceland. I heard my sister saying, "Yes. She's in." And my first guess was that it was one of the women from the chapel, since my mother was Vice President of the Women's Christian Fellowship.

I was sitting, my back to the door, when I felt a tap on my shoulder. Before turning I noticed that my mother's eyes were fixed above me, and she had a girlish look on her face. So I turned. "Chika!" I blurted, unable to hide my surprise. I heard him say good evening to my mother, who asked him to sit. There was a flurry of questions and confusion in my head.

My mother, when she was in one of her best moods, was a perfect hostess. She conversed with Chika, asking his name, and when she heard he was Chika she asked what part of the southeast he hailed from. He said Abia, Ohafia specifically. I felt ashamed that I hadn't asked for any other detail apart from his first name, and my mother had not even asked for his surname. I was sitting where I had been when he arrived; my sister went to the kitchen to get him a drink, as was our custom for any visitor.

He did not turn to look at me once while he conversed with my mother, and he said things that made her giggle. He spoke about how he had been corrupted by Yoruba food, and my mother laughed, and agreed with him that Igbo food had less oil than Yoruba food. And he said that in life there were those better than you, in everything; as Igbo food was better than Yoruba food, so was Calabar food better than Igbo food. My mother did not laugh much at this. Apparently, she hadn't thought of food as a source of wisdom, as an important anecdote that typified life.

My mother said, "You are very smart, Chika." She was the kind of person who said what she thought, using the exact words in which the thought had come to her head. I envied her ability to do this. And when she said it to Chika, I felt somewhat happy, as though the praise wasn't for him alone—I felt proud that she thought my visitor was smart. "You know, Chika, you're the first Igbo man she is bringing to this house. All those Yoruba boys she had brought home, I don't know where they are now." Chika chuckled at this, almost spitting his juice.

"You were the one that brought her home the other day?" she asked.

"Yes."

"Oh. Good. I like this." My mother looked at me, winked, and smiled.

I shook my head, nervous, wondering what the right feeling for a situation like that was—my mother's approval for a man I barely knew. Chika cleared his throat and asked my mother, "Ma, I came to take her out, talk with her for some time."

My mother said, annoying me immensely in the process, "She's not a baby, Chika."

When we were in his car, he told me, "I came to say I am sorry, again."

I replied, "You shouldn't be sorry. I should be sorry too."

"We are two sorry people then." He took my hand, held it tightly till I had to scream in delight, and pain. "That's how sorry I am." We laughed together at this.

I asked him, "What's your surname?"

"Igwe." I nodded. I expected him to ask me the same, but he said, "I want to know little of you. I'm in passing. A traveler whose trip is ending does not take too much from the place he is leaving." I saw that he was looking at me while he said this. I wanted him to hold my hand as he had done before, squeeze me until I was left with nothing but craving, for him, for life.

"That's a very cruel thing to say," I replied.

"You're not asking me questions. You're assuming nothing is wrong," he told me, still looking fixedly at me. I supposed he expected me to add things up, but I remembered being bad at math. I took no learning experience from the subject; I couldn't calculate a simple formula of existence.

"Is it wrong to assume too much?"

"It's dangerous," he answered.

"It is safe."

"I get your point, then."

"Good. I will assume you know me very well. I will assume all is well with you."

We agreed that he should take me to his house, so we could watch a movie together. His house was at Omole Estate, outside the campus. While he drove, he told me he had just listened to Colbie Caillat's "The Little Things." I told him I didn't know the name, I didn't listen much to music that wasn't gospel. He said he respected that decision, but pointed out that what appealed to him was the title, and he was ready to take note of little things, like yawning, farting, spitting, hissing, wearing a shoe, the color of his sponge, the number of text messages on his phone. I laughed till my sides ached. He didn't laugh, but smiled, and I realized he was indulging me, smiling so that my laughter did not become questionable.

His house was modest, but spacious. My first question was, "You've never gotten married?" He smiled, and said, "No. Thank you. I'm only thirty-eight." I sat. His chairs were covered in soft leather. He had a television, a satellite dish receiver, a DVD player. On the wall hung a small photograph of a woman, most likely his mother.

The movie I chose was *The Oxford Murders*, and he said he loved very few things about the movie, especially because one of the protagonists spoke of cancer too compassionately, as though it wasn't a fact of life for many people. I shushed him jokingly, warning him not to run commentary for me, I wanted to see the movie and draw conclusions for myself.

By the time the movie was over, Chika was asleep on one of the chairs. He snored lightly; it was the first time I loved hearing snoring. I wanted to wait until he woke, but I looked at his clock and saw that it was a few minutes before 7:30 p.m. I stirred him. Surprised, he asked, "Is it morning?"

I sat beside him, smiling, willing myself to lull him to sleep again. "No."

Then he said, "Let me take you home."

I did not want him to say that; I had never had sex with Mark or Babatunde, and it had never appealed to me as an affirmation of affection, of the kind of love Babatunde would have called deep. Now, even though I wasn't sure Chika loved me, or wanted a romantic interaction, I felt sex was needed. But I knew I was reacting too much to the affection he'd fed me that evening, and he did not even seem to be in the mood for it.

He straightened his shirt, stood up and looked at his watch. "We should go now."

I sat still, wondering if my face did not disclose, even faintly, my mood. When he saw that I hesitated, he sat beside me, close enough that I could feel the warmth of his skin. He asked me, "Did you enjoy the movie? I'm sorry I slept."

I told him I enjoyed the movie; I couldn't tell him I was thinking about having sex with him. I stood without him asking me to, again. I hugged him and told him thank you. His hands patted me lightly on my back, so that I understood that my sudden hug had surprised him, or that he was unprepared for physical touch, or that he assumed physical touch would break down every little thing we had built so far.

But he hugged me after I released him from my grasp. We remained in each other's embrace for a minute, or two, a personal record for me. I had the feeling it wasn't a mere pre-sexual embrace, or the testing of waters by prospective lovers. I had the feeling that for him it went beyond the body, beyond the nervousness I felt while in his arms, the longing for a kiss. It could be that, for him, a kiss, or even intercourse, meant more than sensuality. When he gently released himself, there were tears in the corners of his eyes. I asked no question, not wanting to jeopardize future embraces.

While Chika drove me home we shared a silence that seemed worthy. I looked at him, at his clean-shaven chin, his receding hairline, and I perceived he thought of his body too lightly, that even if we'd had sex it would mean nothing to him; he'd pass over it like he was brushing his teeth, or farting.

VII

I went to Papa again. There were times, such as the night of Chika's embrace, when I held the memories of both men in my head, considering the relationship I had with each as an unfolding quest. But my return to Papa was partly the result of a bout of boredom that had overcome me—perhaps emptiness—the day after the minute-long embrace with Chika. I couldn't even muster the energy to keep my Twitter diary. I'd post a Tweet, re-read it and see that my own musings bored me, so I'd delete it. Eventually I just stopped trying. It seemed that I sought another form of embrace, this time one that would be wrapped around my soul. Papa's unfinished story would have to suffice.

He was wearing reading glasses when I came in and seemed disturbed, irritated even. I hoped it wouldn't last.

Nothing in his appearance changed when I sat. "I woke up with an incongruous thought. That I'd die being hated by my son."

He spoke so well, used words only an educated person could use. Then I shushed myself, seeing that I was thinking tangentially again, concerned about his use of words, not his pain. "Why did you think such a thing?"

"Because I did!" he snapped.

I felt sorry for him, and for myself. I looked at his hair, noticing for the first time that he was not bald, that his hair wasn't completely grey. "I'm sorry," I said, conscious that being sorry did not save things, ultimately.

"We left his mother. I took him and we left his mother. She was sick, something really dreadful, maybe they'd say it was AIDS now. We didn't know what it was. She was losing weight as though her life was being sucked away. I took her to our home-town, left her in our family house, and I left with my son, seeking a life that wasn't hovering around death. I wanted to live. So we came to Lagos, that city of multitude devilish possibilities. I found a job in one of the secondary schools, teaching English." He opened the refrigerator, removed and took a swig from his gin bottle. He turned to me and smiled briefly. When he returned the bottle with his previously shaky hands now still, he lost every trace of that smile.

"They did not even tell us when she died, or when they buried her," he said. Then he took away his reading glasses. "I remember that moment when the news was broken in our living room as the moment when my son began to hate me—I had brought him to a motherless life. I was the one whose decision had spoiled things. We never argued about this; he's the kind of person whose feelings could be frozen."

He didn't seem to want to say more. I couldn't even tell what I had learned. A larger scheme was yet to unfold. I was holding only bits of subplots.

"That's all, really. I retired and couldn't pay for a house, you know the pension worries. He was out of Lagos, but he came for me, brought me to his house. Then he found me unbearable, and brought me here."

"Where's he now?"

"I've said he's here in Ife!" he barked.

I didn't remember hearing his son was in Ife.

"Mosun, could you go now and return later? I will be hap-pier next time."

I said yes and rose from the seat. Meetings with him always ended at the threshold of a story, of an insight into his past. But that afternoon it really seemed that when I returned he'd reveal his plot.

VIII

Early the morning after I visited Papa, Chika called to say he was going to stay indoors mostly. I asked him why and he said he would send a text. I looked at my phone expectantly, alert for his message, wondering what would happen if there were no phones, no technology, if our brief interaction wouldn't fall apart for lack of weight.

His message finally arrived at noon. "I have cancer. I am dying. I should have told you."

I thought immediately of his face, that I should have seen the cracks in it, and maybe on the rest of his body. I stood up from my bed and sat down immediately, then stood again, then sat. I went on like that. I soon began to pace the room. Then I picked up my phone and dialed his number. He said, "Hello," and I said nothing, hoping the seconds would not count. I took the phone off my ear and held it in my palm, watching the seconds pass. He hung up but I kept holding the phone. I wanted some reminder, a scene that would represent the moment, though one unrelated to it. I felt it could be my phone; if I held it long enough, I would create a permanent feeling, so that when I remembered there would be something to cling to.

I asked my mother for her car and drove to his house. When he opened the door, I expected to perceive a disgusting smell, but it was his aroma as I remembered. I hugged him as soon as he opened the door and I heard him sniffling. When I disentangled myself from his embrace I saw that he was crying. He bent, holding his knees with his hands, and he cried freely. I stood, unable to speak, knowing that no words would be appropriate. I heard him say, "I don't want you to see me like this. You must go. Please." But I decided that I would hear him as though he was shouting from a distance. He was still bent over when I walked past him and went into his living room and wept too.

"I have started to feel the pain already," he said, smiling. After crying, I pulled shut his curtains to avoid the light. I needed to make his living room feel like a cave, a hideout, a spot where one could retreat from the brightness of life.

I said nothing in response to what he said about the pain. Instead, I said, "I have heard of people cured from this." He shook his head, and I saw how tired his eyes were, suddenly, and yet his face did not seem as incomplete as before. Perhaps I was being a bad judge, seeing things wrong.

"You know, there are times when the sun is shining and a light rain is falling at the same time. In South Africa they call it a 'monkey's wedding.'"

"Shut up."

"Maybe a month, now."

"Shut up. Really. Shut up."

"You believe in miracles?"

"Yes. Yes."

"What does it take for a miracle to happen?"

"Faith."

"It is not a question of faith for me. I can have faith. It's just I'm not ready to put up the fight for faith. I have let go too much."

"When did you know?"

"That day we met."

"You were talking about getting wet."

"Yes."

I cried again. I should have been strong for him; he was being strong for me. He told me again to leave. This time he said he didn't want me to return. I said shut up again, and he cried again, leaving me to find the right words. "You're making me cry too much," he said. "Please go. Please." I moved to go and he didn't budge. In my mother's car I expected to see his figure from the rear-view mirror. He was not there. Then I realized that perhaps he didn't need me. I wasn't sure.

IX

I drove to the Home after I left Chika, still confused. I might have been acting instinctively, going for a chat with Papa, an older man who might understand dying. He had become my friend in an unexpected manner. He was the kind of person who, without reason, was endearing. Or perhaps he was endearing because, aside from Chika, no one else had mattered to me in the previous weeks. He kept to his word, being happier this time. I was the one who felt sad.

"You don't look happy," he said, sitting up on his bed.

"Yes," was all I said.

"You want to tell me what's bothering you?"

He sounded like a grandfather. I hated the sound of, pity. "I don't want to tell you." I felt like a baby.

"Okay," he said, reclining on his bed, his back resting on the bed frame. "You know, since the last time you were here, I've been thinking of reconciliation. With my son."

I was becoming angry at the turn of events, at cancer intercepting bliss. But there was no malice in his voice. I felt disconnected, like I was there for no reason.

"You could go to him, then," I said, only out of courtesy.

Papa said nothing for a while. Then he told me, "I want you to be the middle person. You know, fix a meeting."

I didn't deem myself qualified.

"You're the only person I talk to here. I can't live like this, die haunted by hate."

"I'll do it," I said.

"Thank you," he said, smiling. "What's his name?"

"Chika," he said, "Chika Igwe."

I told Papa I was leaving, tears had filled my eyes.

"You know him?"

But I said nothing. I exited silent as a stone, but weeping.

X

My phone beeped while I was driving home, all the while wiping my eyes. The message read, "I have resigned my job. I want to take photographs of the university. Everywhere."

I imagined how he felt, what dying meant to him, whether it had changed his convictions about death. I knew we would never talk about death in that sense, mentioning it directly. We would talk about it euphemistically. This could be because I wasn't brave enough—because his braveness was in keeping the subject tucked in his mind, far away from my reach.

I thought of my brother with cancer, my father with cancer, Mark or Babatunde with cancer, or every other man I knew.

At home I went immediately to my laptop and got online. I googled "cancer in men." There were Wikipedia articles, links to medical journals, news sites that reported the prevalence of the sickness. I scanned through the results, with the hope of finding any that excluded cancer from the list of terminal illnesses. It was a faint hope, like the memories of the caress of a resplendent cloth. I stared at the search results for as long as twenty minutes, scrolling through the options again and again. Then I remembered Christ Embassy, a church known for miracles. I found the church website and under "Testimonies" I searched the list for the name of any man who had been healed of cancer. There was one, Ufere Ugboma. I returned to Google and typed his name in the search bar. The results were few; the second result was his

Facebook account, the third a Twitter account with no tweets. So I logged into Facebook and typed his name in the search bar. There were five Ufere Ugbomas. There was no photo for him on the Christ Embassy page, so it was impossible to tell which one on Facebook account was the Christ Embassy Ugboma. I decided to send a friend request to all five of them, adding the same personal message: "Thank God for your miracle. Did you do anything special?"

I remembered Papa, what he'd asked of me, how things had become stranger still, how I had held separate friendships with father and son, friendships that were now converging. I did not feel strong enough to contemplate the dynamics of coincidence; all I could think of was how a living man had become a dying man. I knew that when I felt strong enough to go to Chika again, I would mention his father—who knew where that would lead.

I took advantage of being online and logged into my Twitter account. I had to capture this moment.

None of the Ufere Ugbomas replied to my Facebook message or accepted my friend request. I waited for three days before concluding that I wasn't going to get any response, that it had been a foolish idea from the start. In those three days I did not speak to Chika, but he sent dozens of text messages, describing the photos he was taking. In one of his messages, the longest, he wrote about the various snapshots he had taken of the Natural History Museum being built on campus. He had taken eighty-one shots of the building in all. He wished I could see the pictures, but he wasn't sure I would be interested.

I sent no response to his messages; I was not going to be complicit. My duty was to make him believe that he would not die, that for him there was a wide gulf between mortality and immortality, that as long as I lived he lived. But it was a difficult thing to do. I was running out of options.

The days climbed into each other and it became a week since I had last seen him. But he kept sending his messages, so that I became enraged and stopped reading them. He was being unfair to me; I wanted him to stay and he wanted to leave, taking photos meant he wanted to leave something behind, and telling me of the photos made me a part of his leaving plan, as though he didn't know how much he already meant to me.

XI

Chika hugged me first, smiling heartily, asking how I had been. I said nothing in response. He sat beside me, putting his hands around my shoulders, asking again how I was. He had a new smell. "You won't talk to me? Did I offend you?" He was serious now, too serious.

"No. No."

"Why didn't you ask me to come for you? I don't drive much these days but I can come. I would have managed." I turned to look at him, hoping he would see how stupid his words sounded. I saw that he was smiling, and there were tears around his eyes, and I remembered how it was possible for the sun to shine while the rain fell.

"There was a debate in *Monocle* about digital and analogue photography. Some people prefer the darkroom to the laser printer. I think I prefer that. If I had my way I would have printed all my pictures in the darkroom."

I waited for the right moment to tell him about his father. When he said nothing about the photographs again, I said, "I met your father."

He reacted only with a frown, taking his hand off my shoulder, asking, "What did he say?"

"He wants to meet with you."

"Did you tell him?"

"I didn't tell him."

"I don't want him to know." He stood and walked into his room.

I followed. "You should meet him. Really."

He sat on his bed, still frowning, and I could see that he was not looking at me, not thinking of me; it seemed he was remembering. "When I'm gone you'll take things to him, please. I don't want anything to do with him."

"You want to go holding hate in your heart."

He looked at me, his eyes filled with unshed tears. I went to the bed and sat beside him, reached and brought his head to my chest. "No, I don't want to see my father. No."

"He told me what happened, about your mother."

"I'm sure he told you lies."

"How can you be sure?"

He shook his head and it bumped my left breast. He raised his head, seeming embarrassed. But he drew his face to mine and I kissed him. Our mouths locked briefly, then he withdrew. When I looked at him there was no surprise in his face.

"There were days I dreamed of kissing you. But I can't do that to you, use your body to achieve a fleeting satisfaction."

"That's not what it is to me."

"I can't love you the normal way. Death has enslaved me."

"I don't care about the normal way. If you love me maybe you'll be well."

He shook his head, closed his eyes, sliding the fingers of his left hand into mine.

"I was misdiagnosed several times for close to four years. It's prostate cancer, but they thought it was benign prostate enlargement. When they found out it was too late. So you see, it's not a simple sickness."

193

I knew that any response I gave would be inappropriate. I couldn't speak of the possibility of a miracle or even the almightiness of God. "You should see your father," I said, devoid of other words.

"There are things," he said, "that do not matter in the end. I have thought of many last things. Not seeing my father. If I see him I don't think anything will have changed."

I began to cry. This time he drew my head to his chest, saying sorry. I thought of how our roles had reversed; he was now the stronger one.

XII

For the next five days I committed to my Twitter diary, sending messages into the ether five times a day. But this time I focused on other parts of my life, as a way to distract myself from Chika and his father. There were other facets of my life, after all. I lived a duality, much like a monkey's wedding. Sunshine and rainfall.

March 3
Today the Choirmaster announced he wasn't going to contest the coming elections. I wasn't sad, it was simply information.

There were those around me who suggested he was resigning because of the attack on him, more or less like he'd been threatened to step down

Some pointed accusing fingers at Mr. Lekan, who up until then was a harbinger of progress, the one we looked up to when clichés annoyed us

I watched Mr. Lekan, the accused, who steadied his gaze on whatever was in front of him, as though the Choirmaster was a bad vision

It rained after the rehearsals, and I walked in the rain to my mother's car, afraid of being considered irrelevant because of my silence

March 4

My mother got a call from Professor Clara, as they were close friends.
She said the Professor had asked that she come with me, if possible

When we got to her house she was in her night-dress, and she showed
us a calabash of charms she found on her doorstep, which she didn't fear

And my mother, ever the panicking woman, asked if she'd offended
anyone, because charms often work, that even Christians are also affected

But Professor Clara said she had a feeling it had to do with contesting
for Choirmaster, that she'd heard how Mr. Lekan boasted of victory

And she asked me if I was on her side, if I would vote for her, not mind-
ing her age, or qualification, making me say yes, though in doubt

March 5

Muna, the assistant Chaplain, called me. He spoke without pauses, as
though he recorded his voice, like a caller tune,

He'd asked me to call him Muna, not Reverend, and I obliged him
because I heard his past was something to forget, a story of heavy words

And he wanted us to have a drink, at Motel Royale, and I responded that
I would have to think about it, seeing as I was recovering from Chika

He told me to take my time, that he wasn't in a hurry, but that he'd look
forward to a yes, because he was becoming aware of changes

"Change" was like a bad memory, like a dangerous zone being revisited,
failure being re-sought and I, began to think of recoiling from him

March 6

I took Muna to Chika's house, where we met Chika's absence, and it was
then we heard from his neighbor that he was in the hospital

I didn't go to the hospital, afraid of the inevitable, nor did I try to speak with him on the phone though his name played in my head always

I spoke with Chika once when he was in the hospital, he called and said he wanted to hear my voice, an item in his very last wish list

Papa wanted me to see him, and though it was not my wish, seeing that the past was not past, I obliged, hoping to avoid the pain in his gaze

We talked about nothing in particular, only asking about our welfares, only supporting our joint grief with the nuisance of daily life

March 7

Papa told me, yesterday that he saw Chika's body before it was buried, that they didn't believe he was Chika's father, he had no proof

I thought of proofs, a proof that the events unfolding in the choir were hinged on a larger scheme of things, but I'm no good at math

I didn't want to think of Chika, how in the end I was too weak to go to him, how I only harbored his face in my mind, rinsing it of all dying

And I began to feel guilty of not touching him one last time, because one last time meant a towering stone of the past, an unmoving vestige

I am aware of unsaid things, aware that, like the Choirmaster election, much ado could be built from little things, big things, or both

Seven

A FATHER'S SON

I

When my son came back to Ife, I saw he was growing a beard. He is usually clean-shaven, only occasionally does his chin have stubble. But when he returned that early evening in August, I saw his beard had been growing awhile, was even drooping a few inches. I hugged him first before I asked him about his beard.

"It's the sign of change, Daddy," he replied, laughing in his usual manner. I missed being with him. I told him so. He nodded without indicating that he missed me too. It looked as though he knew how I felt about his absence but could not reckon with the fact.

I told him about the changes in my life. The Chapel had extended my tenure for another three years, making it impossible for me to think of another destination. "Ife is beautiful," he said. There was an uneasy silence between us. He waited for me to speak before he responded—this was particularly unnerving.

"You've changed," I told him.

"No," he said, "I feel like my life is in slow motion or even stationary. We have to pray for the change to come."

I looked at him closely when he said that. My son had my face. There were lines on his forehead that spoke of my life. It did not matter whether he was expressing worry or joy; the lines all showed the same, like they showed on my face. In this way, he was the extension of my life, so that when people saw him they spoke as though I was not his father, as though our semblance were from different sources. As though I could not be found at his origin.

"The change will come," I said and patted his back.

My touch alerted him. He stood up and announced that he had to use the bathroom, that he was pressed to shit. I watched him move. His jeans were slim, fitting him tightly. His shirt was wrinkled from traveling long on the bus. I told him again that I missed him.

"I missed you too, Daddy," he said and walked away out of the room. His saying that he missed me too made me feel old. I stood as he walked away and went to the dining room where there was fruit on a tray. I peeled one of the bananas and ate it halfway, placing the second half back on the tray. I opened the refrigerator and took out a bottle of water. I was tempted to drink from the bottle, but I remembered that my son was back. I wasn't alone anymore. So I found a cup and filled it.

He called to me from the bathroom. "How's Uncle Francis?" In return, I shouted, "He has his doctorate now."

It took him a while before he said, "That's great."

I went back to the living room and waited for him to join me. There were things that were yet to be said.

II

When his mother died, we still lived in Port Harcourt. I worked then with Bible Alliance, an interdenominational ministry with branches across the world. Our mission was to help distribute Bibles and Christian literature, and teach how the Bible should be read.

She died of cancer, but I was too inexperienced to know what it was. My son, too, was too young to know his mother was dying. I sometimes feel he took our visits to her in the hospital with levity—as though he was visiting the museum or an amusement park. I told him the usual words—your mother has gone to

Heaven. I remember he nodded, then he smiled; then he said he wanted a Capri Sun.

III

When he came out of the bathroom, I asked my son what his plans were.

"I'm going to Mali." He had just finished law school, had come home after his final exams, and was awaiting his results. Mali sounded like a foolish idea. But I had given him too much liberty when he was younger; it was too late to take it away now. I had allowed him to travel alone from Abuja to Lagos when he was only eleven, for instance. It was, therefore, our unspoken rule to make his life into one with inexhaustible boundaries.

"Mali?"

"Yes."

"For what?"

"A photography expedition."

"That is very interesting." I asked him when he was leaving.

"Tomorrow," he replied.

When he said this, I thought I would slap him, remind him that he was all I had. But it was impossible. I could not remember the last time I had hit him.

IV

When I met my son's mother, she was twenty-five and I was twenty-two. She said she wanted only one child. I agreed. We were both from large families—hers was polygamous. My father had ten children, including me. What we wanted for our lives were large thinking spaces, room enough for expression, space to breathe.

And we got it. Our son was born two months premature. So my first instinct was to hate him. I hated the fact that he had rushed out of my wife. But the nurses said premature babies grew up to become intelligent. My son grew up to be intelligent. At twenty-two he finished law school. He told me he wanted to get his PhD at twenty-five.

V

"I don't think you should go to Mali," I told him. By this time, I felt like pulling him by his beard until blood ran from his eyes. He was taking me for granted. He stood and did not argue with me. There was a knock on the door. I did not want to see anyone. There was a wedding at the Chapel the next day, and since it was the Vice Chancellor's daughter, I was receiving a lot of attention. I heard my son say I was in. The Vice Chancellor entered and my son excused himself.

He returned when I was alone. "I'm going to Mali, Daddy. I have already concluded my plans. It's too late now."

I shook my head. "There's nothing like that. You're just back from school. You need some rest."

He shook his head as I had shaken mine. "I don't feel like resting. I feel like doing something. I feel like moving."

"That's unacceptable."

"It's acceptable to me."

"I see. I don't matter anymore."

"Daddy."

I considered his words as though they were water and I could swim. He felt like moving. We had moved all his life, given my work with Bible Alliance and later the Presbyterian Church. He was born in Akure—then we moved to Port Harcourt, then Lagos, then Ife. Ife would be our longest stay, six years so far. I had hoped that he'd start practice in Lagos or Ibadan and that we'd be close.

"How long?"

"Twenty one days."

He had the habit of counting days and I had the habit of counting weeks. He'd call from school and say one hundred and seventy days were left. I hated details. They trivialized life.

"You'll be gone for three weeks?"

"Yes."

He won me over. The next morning, I hugged him until he pushed me gently aside.

VI

His mother told me to take care of him. "He's going to be a lively boy. He's going to want too much from life. He's going to want to put too much into life. But you should take him as he is."

When she said this, I remembered an earlier conversation. She said I was a low-getter, I demanded too little from existence. "You live life as if it has no color." I did not argue with her. She was in the advanced stage of her sickness—in those days I treated her with the transience she demanded as she confronted the inevitability of her passing. I used to hate looking at her face. Her face used to remind me of too many undreamed nightmares; it used to make me think of the evil I was yet to experience. Even earlier memories of our love would not shake the feeling of undreamed nightmares.

The night before she died she spoke of her plans, of the first request she'd make to God when she got to Heaven. She'd ask for a logbook to record the life and times of our son. I cried when she said that. She held my face, wiped my tears with her bony fingers, an unforgettable touch that wiped away the undesired memory. I have never shaken the thought that on her last night I slept with my head on her shoulder. Or the thought of how she gathered the strength to bear me.

VII

I had to push my son aside when he returned from Mali. He pressed me too close to himself, so that the stench of his sweat hit me with force. "Daddy!" He screamed.

I looked at him; his beard was gone. So the first words I said to him were, "You've shaved your beard."

He asked, "Is it nice?"

I said, "Wonderful. How are you?" He nodded that he was okay. I shook my head, smiled, and looked away. You know how it is when you feel excited beyond description, and the excitement is not in your head but in your belly. That was how I felt when I saw my son. I noticed that he hung a camera over his shoulders. "You bought this?"

"Ah," he said. "Yes. Mali is a beautiful place. You should go there sometime. We have too many stereotypes. We are too used to Nigeria, you know."

I did not see the wisdom in his words. As far as I was concerned, I was through with moving.

So at the earliest opportunity, when he sat at the dining table, eating, I said to him, "You know I am almost through with my doctorate. I will apply for a position next year."

He smiled. Because I was sitting next to him, I saw how quickly the lines on his forehead formed, and how quickly they disappeared. He stood, his food was eaten halfway. "I want to take a photo of you." He walked to his room and came out with his camera. I was shaking my head, saying no to him. But he brushed aside my concerns, and went ahead and took the photo.

"I don't like this, you know?"

When he saw that I was serious, he dropped the camera on the dining table, and said, "I'm sorry."

"It's just that I don't know what you want to do with your life. You're giving me no clue."

The way he looked at me, I felt he was going to say, "I have my life to live," but he asked me, "Is it a doctorate you want?"

I said, "Yes. I don't want to leave Ife."

He only said, "Okay." He picked his camera and walked into his room. His food was still half-eaten. I drew the plate to me, and began to eat what my son had left.

VIII

When we came to Ife, my son was just through with secondary school. His mother had died twelve years before. I had gotten an appointment as a chaplain with the interdenominational chapel at the university.

My son asked me, "Are you going to get married again?" We had just unpacked our things; young people from the church who had come to help us were in the house, chatting excitedly among themselves. He had asked me openly.

I thought his voice was too loud, and I thought the young people in the living room had heard him. I drew him into my room and we sat on the bed. "Why are you asking?"

"You don't seem to have moved on."

He was sixteen. It was not the age for such intelligence. "What do you mean?" I asked him, hoping my befuddlement was not apparent.

"I don't know, Daddy."

"Is it about this place?"

"No."

"Then what?"

"I don't know. I remember her, sometimes, you know. I didn't even know her."

"Yes," was all I could say. Then I asked him to leave me alone.

I remembered her, too, thinking often that I had not known her—that time had blurred who she was. She had become like a single cell seeking attention in a giant body.

IX

I was dressed before my son was finished. When I went to his room, I found that he was having difficulty choosing which shirt to wear. Aside from the fact that most of his shirts were dirty and rumpled from his journey, I perceived that he was being careful to make the right impression at the farewell dinner.

He finally chose a pink shirt with thin black stripes. "I'll take my camera," he said.

"Sure," I answered. I suddenly felt fatigued. I sat back on his bed. I could sit there forever, have him by my side and remember his mother.

He spoke, intruding into my head, my memory. "Daddy? Are you fine?"

"Oh sure."

"You took your drugs?"

By drugs he meant my supplements—the small tablets I took to enhance my health. They could work for your body, but I did not consider them supplements for the mind. "Yes, I did." I stood and said, "Let's go."

He drove my car—the Chapel's car, which served for both personal and official use. The staff quarters where we lived were an amalgam of various concerns, of various lifestyles. There were those like us, who lived on the intersection between affluence and want, those of us who could not afford to travel overseas for conferences, vacations, fellowships, those whose academic calling thrived on a lackluster lifestyle, the absence of any zeal, magic, or miracle. On the other side of the spectrum were those with international connections, for whom it was a yearly feat to attend conferences at Harvard and Stanford, visit their children in London, and hold fellowships in China. My view of the staff quarters had always been Marxist; I often longed for a revolution, a merging of strata—a redefinition of our lives. In some way, I had hoped that my son would share my ambition. It could be too much to expect him to practice law in Ife. But it could not be too much to want him to be fixed, build his career around Ife, and make us what we longed to be.

"Nothing has changed here," he said.

"Of course. Things do not change."

"The context of things changes."

"What do you mean?"

"Content is fixed, context changes. The way we look at things changes after we move. But what we're looking at is essentially the same."

"I see," was all I said. I loathed the voice with which he spoke, with incalculable omniscience. You know how it feels for a man who has watched his son grow, who must have taught his son, the boy, all that he knows, to watch the boy grow and begin to teach him, the man?

I commended his driving. "Near perfect," I joked.

By then we had parked at Professor Onwudiegwu's house and my attention was divided. The Professor had announced, a week before my son returned and three weeks after delivering his inaugural lecture, that he was relocating to Malta.

"What in God's name?" I asked him. He, like me, remained single after the death of his wife. He had a child, a girl my son's age, named Chinwe. I had asked him if he was sure about Malta. He had said yes, that his daughter was going to remain in Nigeria. She'd relocate to Manchester after a year.

The living room was crammed with a small community of people I knew. I smiled, said hellos, returned greetings, aware of the geniality that was a requisite for my position. My son received an equal amount of compliments. The gospel music of Patty Obasi played in the background. I felt exhilarated; the music charged the atmosphere, gave it more relevance than it would have if it had been Yinka Ayefele or Tope Alabi singing more contemporary Yoruba gospel tunes. I sought Professor Onwudiegwu's attention, and when we met he hugged me tightly. "I will miss you, Reverend," he said.

I nodded, smiled, and told him I would miss him too. When I first arrived he was the Chairman of the Chapel Board; he had helped me find my bearings. In some way, I thought his daughter helped my son stabilize, too. From the corner of my eyes, I searched for my son. I saw that he had found Chinwe; they were chatting. His hands were pocketed, something he usually did when he was nervous. I smiled and carried on the conversation with Professor Onwudiegwu.

Later, just after my son tugged my sleeve and said he would be outside, I went to Chinwe. After we exchanged pleasantries, I asked her what her plans were. "I will be in Ife for another year. I'll take my time, think of things to do." Her voice was velvety. I could have asked her for specific details of what she'd do, but I felt inclined to have a different conversation, especially one that had something to do with my son.

"I knew about you and my son."

"Oh."

"Sure. I thought it was perfect, you know."

She looked closely at me, directly for the first time.

"He is a good person. I felt, sometimes, that I didn't deserve him."

I was taken aback. "Why's that?"

She smiled as though I would not understand. "Ah. It's difficult to explain, Sir. He's too much for me."

I was groping. "It's just perfect. Both of you, here, from the east, a new Igbo generation."

She frowned, seeming surprised that I had such considerations. I, too, felt weightless, ashamed of my age. "We didn't think of that at all. I told him we could not continue. He has not told you?"

I shook my head, ashamed again. "We don't talk about such things." She looked hesitant to say much more. And because I felt the conversation had ended, anyway, I told her to feel free to speak to me anytime, especially now that her father was leaving.

X

My son's mother knew she was going to die. So she asked me if I was going to marry again, after she was gone. I laughed and told her she wasn't going to die. God was a healing balm. If I had had doubts, it would have been easier to accept her death, to accept that I was going to be a widower. But it was the period of my life when I accepted faith wholesale, and successfully doubted all my doubts. She died, nonetheless.

When she pushed further I told her, "I don't know. It's a question of whether or not you die." She shook her head, and said I was being evasive, which was proof of my promiscuity and infidelity. I laughed. She laughed too, so that I wasn't sure whether she was joking or serious about doubting my fidelity.

And it was right then that I decided not to marry again. I wanted to prove her wrong. I wanted to allay her fears about our son. She once said she'd make a bad stepmother; there was a widower who had asked her to marry him, before she met me. She said if she had married him she would have been wicked to his children—that she wanted too much of life to spend what little she had on what wasn't hers. Now that she wasn't going to be around to spend her life on what belonged to her, she was delegating me to do so, for her sake.

I felt she was asking too much of me.

XI

I talked to my son about Chinwe. He shook his head in disbelief that I would even broach the topic.

"That's a long story, Daddy." He was smiling, evading my gaze. "Look at me," I said, sounding serious, so that he'd understand the weight of the matter. "What happened?"

He shook his head again, failing to look at me. "She left me, Daddy. I didn't leave her."

I said, "But, she still loves you." I felt his restraint, his discomfort that we were talking about Chinwe; his love life up until that moment had been off limits. I saw he was more comfortable with the barricade in place.

"Let's not talk about this, Daddy." He stood up from his bed. "Let's just say our devotions here," he said. I nodded, he walked to get his Bible and our book of devotional readings.

We read the story of Abraham, the part where he left his father to discover a land God would show him. When it was time for commentaries, I took the liberty to speak of how standard Abraham's faith was, how incisive, and perhaps how dissident. Later, I'd conclude that it was a mistake to speak in such fashion about something I disliked. And it would be one of a number of instances when I preached of themes I questioned. My son said he had no comments on the chapter we'd read. So we prayed. He led the prayers, committing our engagements to the Lord, our future, forthcoming things. I liked the passion in his voice, the deep-seated concern for our lives, especially his.

"So, what are your plans?" I asked, still sitting on his bed.

"Ah," he sighed, "I applied for a photography residency at the University of Pennsylvania. I'll be informed of the Board's decision next week. If it's favorable, I'll leave in a month's time."

I shook my head, scratched my eyes, something I did when I was uncomfortable. "You didn't tell me all this. You made your decision without asking me for an opinion? It's ridiculous, really. That's to say the least."

"I'm sorry, Daddy."

"So what happens to Law?"

"I don't know. It's never been an option for me."

"Oh, right. I guess we just wasted our time."

"No. It wasn't."

"Then what was it?" I raised my voice. "Tell me!"

He bent his head. Unlike other arguments we'd had, it didn't appear to me that I was being too harsh, too pushy. I felt right.

"You didn't tell me to study Law. I chose it myself."

"I gave you too much freedom, I see."

"Daddy, please."

"Please what? It's your life, I guess. I don't fit in."

"Daddy."

I stood and left his room. I could feel his plea, right in the part of my head that throbbed. But I wouldn't listen. For me, it was a fight.

XII

The Chapel organized an outreach to Ilesha Prison. My son went with us. Our conversations had been perfunctory since I had walked out of his room. He carried his head bent around me. I didn't want to care, but I did. He sat with me in the front seat of the bus. I knew it was his method of initiating a truce. It would have been easier if our fight had been caused by simpler matters—a shirt he had failed to iron, a call he had failed to make, an email he did not send. But it was a more complicated matter. I could not fathom convincing him otherwise, and this was frustrating. For the visit the Head of the Prison Outreach Committee paired me with my son; everyone laughed at what they considered a perfect team. Although, I wished I felt differently, I cannot deny how apt it felt. We were led to the prisoners; a narrow hallway demarcated two long cells. The inmates were cramped in either of the large cells.

My son spoke to the prisoners about freedom. You know how powerful a word can be, how it can strike your heart like a punch aimed at your life? He told the prisoners how freedom of the soul was more important than freedom of the body, and how the former was more glorifying. I saw that one of the prisoners was wiping tears from his face. I turned to look at my son. I was proud of him; it was no different from the time he'd won a prize at his convocation ceremony, when his classmates had roared our surname. The prisoner who had cried wrote his name on a sheet of paper and gave to my son, asking him to remember him in prayers—he had been there for seven years, and would be going to court the following Monday for the second time.

When we were alone, I told him, "God bless you, boy."

This time he did not bend his head. He looked at me, straight in the eye, and said, "Thank you, Daddy." When we joined the others, there was a lady my son spoke with, in the same nervous way I had seen him speak with Chinwe. Her name was Aanu. She sang in the choir.

He did not sit with me on the way back to the Chapel. He sat beside Aanu. Often, when I looked at them through the rear-view mirror, I saw them smile as they chatted, looking out of the window together. I feared the outcome of their conversation; she was a Yoruba girl.

XIII

My son confirmed my fears. First, he told me the Board had been favorable; he'd join four other photographers in Pennsylvania for a one-year residency. After that he wished to go to England for his graduate school. Second, he told me he had asked Aanu out and was certain that they'd get married. The information came out in rapid sentences, like a bad meal being eaten hurriedly to avoid the taste. Yet, I did not want to avoid its taste. I wanted to savor the words, to take in my son's derailment.

"How long have you known Aanu?"

"Two months." He was avoiding my gaze, disappearing from the intensity of my curiosity.

"And you're certain you'll marry her?" I asked, hoping the sarcasm in my voice made a lot of noise.

"All things being equal, yes."

"How old are you that you are speaking of marriage?" He did not answer me. I was mocking him, taking away his confidence, or so I hoped. "You're going away for a year?"

This time I spoke to him in Igbo, as I sometimes did, to which he responded in English. "Yes. Pennsylvania."

I nodded. "How are you going to cope?" I asked, in Igbo.

"They will provide accommodation and a monthly stipend."

"I hate it when I speak to you in Igbo and you answer me in English. It's insulting." He looked flummoxed, as though I was speaking in a language he had tried so much to understand but failed.

"I'm sorry," he said.

"Just go. Just leave me. That's what you want."

"Daddy."

"Just leave me and get married to a Yoruba girl."

I began to cry right in front of my son, thinking suddenly that my wife would have considered me weak, incapable of my son's life. My son did not come close to me. He stood for a moment—then he walked out of the room. I sat on my bed and wiped my tears, wishing that I could cry longer.

XIV

We didn't speak of his plans until he was ready for Pennsylvania. I paid for his fare when he had to go to Lagos for his visa, and I gave him money to shop. There was an informal truce between us on the matter, although I knew that the cord was too weak and our swords too sharp to remain sheathed.

A week before he was to leave, Aanu visited us at home. My son said he invited her to help us cook dinner, to add a different flavor to our meal. I kept my displeasure to myself. Her coming was an open affront to my wishes for my son, an affront to my love—she was ripping a scar that hadn't been there earlier. But I obliged him, given how informally our truce had been initiated, and how much of a failure our ceasefire could otherwise be.

She wore a black gown without sleeves, her arms were the color of mahogany. The gown was not particularly short; it ended slightly below her knees. But the image of what I could see if I happened to be behind her when she bent to pick something—the image of her gown raised to an immoral angle—began to form in my head. I easily concluded that she was a half-chaste girl, one who could give in to sex with mild persuasion.

She cooked beans and fried plantains to go with them. The meal was good, but it had too much oil in it. In her days, my wife had been an excellent cook. She cooked the kind of food you ate and wished your mother had cooked. While we ate, I complimented her. Then I stood, quite abruptly, and told my son to come with me to my room. He hesitated, then glanced at Aanu, who gave him an encouraging nod. Her eyes met mine in the process. I took my eyes away and walked to my room.

My son had anger in his eyes. We were certainly falling apart—our companionship, the connection sons have with their fathers. I felt that what remained was our blood, but that at the right time we could even drain the blood from our kinship.

"You're not going to marry that girl."

"Why not?"

His fighting skills hadn't yet coalesced; I could see he was trying to rebel, but he was unaccustomed to warfare, especially when it was with me. "She's not the kind of girl you should marry," I snapped.

He shook his head. He was unbelievably calm. "Okay," he said. The anger in his eyes had disappeared. When he spoke to me, it was not his voice. "What do you want from me, Daddy?" When I gave him no answer, because I feared I would cry again, he said, "I will tell her I can't marry her." I expected him to say more, but that was all.

I could hear him say to her, "Let's end this thing, right now." I could hear her silence, the shuffling of her feet, the opening of the door, her departure. If I listened carefully I would have heard the wind accompanying her out of the home. But instead, I began to listen to my son whistle "Hello Dolly" on and off. My son often whistled when he was suppressing tears. That evening he whistled and cried at the same time.

XV

When my son turned twenty-five-years old, I sent him a friend request on Facebook, with the hope that he'd respond and speak to me again. I had sent countless emails, searched in vain for his phone number on an online portal, and found none. Then I joined Facebook because I knew most users accessed their accounts daily.

When we got to the airport two years before, as he waited for his flight to America, he told me, "I don't know when I'll be coming home again."

I should have demanded an answer. It would make no sense to expect much and get less. Or so I thought. I could have asked Aanu of him, but she left Ife a month after he left, quitting the Chapel before her departure. When I enquired of her, I was told that she too had been accepted to an American university.

The day after my son left, I went to his room to remember. There was a piece of paper affixed to the door of his wardrobe. Written on the paper was the name of the prisoner who had cried when my son had spoken at our prison outreach. The inmate's name lingered in my memory: Samuel Abraham.

My son called me when he got to America. The caller identity read "unknown." He said, "I've gotten here. I want you to know that I am fine." I told him to keep in touch. But that was the last time I spoke with my son.

XVI

Things are happening so fast that time has passed in a blur. I have been invited to the Choir retreat to give a short talk on the book of Psalms, and I have made small notes in a writing pad—explanations I copied verbatim from Matthew Henry's *Commentary*, the *Lion Guide to the Bible*, and Wellington's *Guide to the Bible*. I lack explanations of my own. As I speak, I notice that many of my listeners are waiting for me to end. Even the Choirmaster, sitting in the front row, is checking his wristwatch.

I say a few more words and end. There are some who look at me in surprise, given that I had announced that I had seven things to say about the book of Psalms and had discussed only four. I ask everyone to stand for prayers. "Lord, you're here with us. Help us to remain with you." There are few who say amen. I do not care. I have the feeling that things are changing so fast I can barely notice. I assume it is time to give in; I have fought for too long.

The Choirmaster announces there will be a break, and that when they return the elections will commence. They are strange, these elections. I have stopped to really care about what decisions are made behind me, as I find it hard to convince even myself that I am the Chaplain.

I think what worries me is the fact that my son has not accepted my friend request on Facebook. It's been close to ten months. Or it could be that I am worried for myself, worried of dying a lonely man's death.

"Sir," the Choirmaster says, "Would you help us conduct the elections?"

I agree. "How do you want them to go?" I have asked the question before I realize he might think I want to favor him. So I say, "How many candidates?" He says there are two of them, just Professor Clara and Mr. Lekan.

"That's alright. We will see how it goes."

I call one of the young people, Oko Egwu. I ask him to get me plain sheets of paper. When he brings them, I divide each sheet into four. I ask him how many choristers there are in all; he says about thirty five. So I make forty little ballots from the sheets he brought. I tell him that after the elections he'll help with the counting. When the choristers gather, I tell them the procedure for the elections. Each person is entitled to a sheet of paper. I am expecting a single letter on each sheet. "A" is for Professor Clara. "B" is for Mr. Lekan.

Then I inform them that Oko Egwu will assist me in counting the ballots. I ask them one final time if we are good to begin.

Oko brings a bucket. It is funny to see that our ballot box is a bucket.

They cast their votes into the bucket. Soon, we start to count. I change the plan. I ask each contestant to step forward. Then I begin to take each sheet from the bucket, opening as I take. I place each sheet that has A in the hands of Professor Clara and the B sheets in Mr. Lekan's hand. Then I ask each of them, starting from Mr. Lekan and ending with Professor Clara, to count their votes out loud.

Professor Clara wins with twenty votes. Mr. Lekan has fifteen. As soon as counting ends, there is a shout of "No!" The voice is Mr. Lekan's. He walks up to the front and hits Professor Clara's hand so that the sheets fall to the floor. Professor Clara seems unperturbed by his act; she's smiling as though she fears nothing. Mr. Lekan screams, startling everyone, a scream that brings immediate silence.

"This is utterly senseless! You'll see what I will do! You will see!" He then storms away.

A general, seemingly unending disquiet descends on the hall. I don't want to imagine the possible consequence of his words. My son had kept his word; he'd said he wasn't sure when he would return, and he has yet to return. Threats were like that, unbelievable at first.

Eight

A RECKONING

Frank was older and he felt wiser, as though he had newly entered into consciousness. Again, his life was interrupted. This time he was called on to talk sanity into Mr. Lekan, the man who lost the choir's elections and then slumped into irrational acts. Once more it was Goody who begged his expertise. They had reunited as a couple.

"The last time I did this," he told her, "my subject disappeared." It brought the past to their thoughts: Ella's whereabouts had remained unknown for the past five years. She had simply walked out of their lives. But Frank, feeling wiser and seeming to possess a sixth sense, always perceived that she wouldn't be gone forever.

Goody persuaded Frank on the matter of Mr. Lekan, believing that what plagued Mr. Lekan resided in his mind, somewhere within reach. "It's always within reach," Frank said, "the problem is usually the distance to be covered."

She pressed further; recently, under the new Choir administration of Professor Clara, Goody had been appointed Head of Welfare. "I told them it wasn't a hospital thing," Goody said to Frank. They were in Frank's house, where she came every day, but never slept. It was a Sunday evening, the day on which Mr. Lekan's irrationality had heightened.

"If it isn't a hospital thing, what is it?"

"I told them the hospital would make him degenerate."

"And what did they say?"

"They agreed. Professor Clara said she'd look after him, see if he gets better. If he doesn't she'll call for professional help."

Frank shook his head. He saw the events of a half-decade ago being replicated, thrown into his plate like vomit. "You demand so much from me," he told Goody.

She folded her arms across her chest and moved away from him. "I left my husband for you. I think you're an ingrate."

She hadn't brought this up, not in the four years since she had relocated to Ife and taken a teaching job at the university's secondary school. That she spoke about leaving her husband for him meant much to Frank; all his logical intuition disappeared when it came to Goody. He drew himself to her, placed his arms around her shoulders. She smiled. The morning she left Chris, as she had told him, was the morning Chris no longer seemed capable of outweighing love with security. The weight of the security he offered had been the reason she'd married him in the first place.

"I don't want to be smeared with irrationality again, never again."

Goody chuckled. "How does one get *smeared* with irrationality?"

Frank chuckled too. "How did you convince them?"

"I spoke like an expert, that's all."

"You're an expert?"

She laughed, drew close to him.

Frank felt lighter in his head, as though her body on his lessened the burden he'd begun to feel. "Where's he now?"

"They took him to the Chapel's boys' quarters. They have a spare room there."

"They should take him to a shrink."

"He's not a patient."

Frank closed his eyes, remembered. "I wish Debbie were here."

"Oh," was all Goody said. Debbie returned to them, often, in single sentences, recollected experiences. She seemed to have deposited her presence in their memories, etched it so that tran-sience became an illusion. This was probably because of the manner of her death—calmly, in her sleep, an expressionless face, as one who was making an endless journey, as one who had an appointment with someone in the afterlife.

"You want me to go to him just like I went to Ella?"

Goody shook her head, "This is not Ella. This is Mr. Lekan."

"Similar circumstances."

"Mr. Lekan is suffering from his own demons."

"And Ella?"

"Maybe a legion of public demons."

"Public demons," he said, laughing, playfully hitting her stomach. But she was serious.

"I think you'll be successful with him."

"I'm not a shrink."

"You said that once. You did well with Ella. She left because she was fine."

"You believe that?"

"Yeah."

He said, "Take me to Professor Clara's house." He felt like an electron, capable of being charged to the point of releasing energy.

Mr. Lekan's irrational acts, which would form the subject of Frank's enquiry, were three-fold. Early on the Sunday following his defeat at the Choir polls, he had gathered puppets together in the Sunday school hall, brought in a piano, and played to the inanimate beings as though they were a congregation. The pup-pets were dressed in their Sunday best, numbering close to fifty. He arranged them on a table in front of the piano. He played his favorite songs for up to five hours, his melodies wafting into the church hall where a normal Sunday service was going on. Many people came to watch, coming and going, but never stopping him.

Only Dr. Addo, famous for his theatrical outburst after reading the essay in the youth publication that denigrated the Choir, came to shout him down. It seemed that everyone was in agreement that it was him, not his puppets, that needed to be shouted down.

His second act came the following Sunday. This time he ran into the church, wearing jeans and an undershirt, and screaming, "I told you I will do it." He ran through the aisle. While he screamed, he flung sheets of paper into the air. They landed on the laps and heads of the congregants, a baptism of paper. And it was also like a baptism of synonyms, for on the sheets was a list of fourteen nonsense words:

Flapdoodle
Applesauce
Buncombe
Bunk
Bunkum
Codswallop
Folderol
Guff
Hogwash
Jive
Junk
Rhubarb
Rot
Frill

It was during this strange show that he was captured by angry ushers who regrettably hadn't anticipated his arrival. They held his hands and his legs and carried him into the vestry, where there was already a woman from the Prayer Team waiting to begin prayers for him. Goody came along with Professor Clara, and while they speculated on what should be done, she remembered Frank had once conferred with a victim of irrationality.

This was the second time that Frank was on a quest to confer healing on harrowing irrationality. This time he was hoping that he could find meaning in what Mr. Lekan had become, rationalize irrationality; for there was always something that moved a man to become a puppeteer and then to make a list of nonsense words. Goody spoke about Mr. Lekan's past, the time before he lost the election—how he had been a fine gentleman, authoritative in matters of contemporary gospel music, a contained elegance evident in his carriage and demeanor. Now he was the one suspected of having sent hoodlums to attack the former Choirmaster, suspected of placing a calabash of charms in Professor Clara's car and on her doorstep.

How could a man, she asked Frank, change so quickly? Professor Clara's house came into view. He told Goody what he had thought of minutes earlier, when he had realized he was a little life in a bigger scheme—"There's always something immeasurable that moves a man to go ashore."

And they were there to find what it was.

Author's Note

The first version of this book was published in Nigeria through the goodwill and vision of Parresia Publishers. Nothing substantial has changed, despite its new title. What's significant, for which I am grateful, is the new North American audience who will now read it. Written by my impressionable 22-year-old self, I remain committed to the book's audacious and restless characters.

For this edition, I am indebted to the generous vision of Shaun Randol, his team at The Mantle, and Victor Ehikhamenor.

My friends and family make my writing life possible, and I thank them.

About the Author

Emmanuel Iduma is a writer and art critic. Born in Nigeria, he cofounded *Saraba Magazine* and has contributed essays and reviews to several magazines and journals. He is also the co-editor of *Gambit: Newer African Writing*. *A Stranger's Pose*, Iduma's book of travel stories and meditations, is forthcoming.